HARD
TO
LOVE

Kendall Ryan is the *New York Times* and *USA Today* bestselling author of contemporary romance novels, including *Hard to Love*, *Unravel Me*, *Resisting Her* and the *Filthy Beautiful Lies* series.

She's a sassy, yet polite Midwestern girl with a deep love of books, and a slight addiction to lipgloss. She lives in Minneapolis with her adorable husband and two baby sons, and enjoys cooking, hiking, being active, and reading. Find out more at www.kendallryanbooks.com

Also by Kendall Ryan

Filthy Beautiful series
Filthy Beautiful Lies
Filthy Beautiful Love
Filthy Beautiful Lust
Filthy Beautiful Forever

Unravel Me series
Unravel Me
Make Me Yours

Love by Design series
Working It
Craving Him
All or Nothing

When I Break series
When I Break
When I Surrender
When We Fall

Hard To Love
Resisting Her
The Impact of You

HARD

TO

LOVE

Kendall Ryan

HARPER

This novel is entirely a work of fiction.
The names, characters and incidents portrayed in it are
the work of the author's imagination. Any resemblance to
actual persons, living or dead, events or localities is
entirely coincidental.

Harper
An imprint of HarperCollins*Publishers*
1 London Bridge Street
London SE1 9FG

www.harpercollins.co.uk

A Paperback Original 2015
1

Copyright © Kendall Ryan 2014

Kendall Ryan asserts the moral right to
be identified as the author of this work

A catalogue record for this book
is available from the British Library

ISBN: 978-0-00-813404-4

Chapter 1

Cade

Dammit. I knew a four-hour erection wasn't normal. I shifted uncomfortably in the cab of my truck and debated what to do. The emergency clinic was open twenty-four hours so that wasn't the problem. It was embarrassment over my condition that had me stalling in the parking lot. But damn, this thing was fucking painful. I tugged on my jeans, trying to create some room and adjusted my erection yet again.

Fuck it. I was going inside.

I stalked across the dimly lit parking lot, trying to walk as normally as possible, but each step tested my sanity.

When I reached the reception desk, an elderly woman looked up and asked if she could help me with something. I struggled to keep a straight face while I explained my problem. She thrust a clipboard of forms at me with a dour expression, not wanting to hear another word. I headed to the waiting room, holding the clipboard in front of my groin.

To make matters worse, Rick, the director I'd been working with on the set, came barging into the emergency room to join me in the waiting area, saying he wasn't about to let one of his actors go through this alone. *Just fucking great.*

Once I turned in the paperwork, I focused on thinking about anything that would tame this monster of a hard-on. The Chicago

1

Bears, how much I hated hospitals —anything non-sexual. Nothing helped. It was full-on throbbing by the time they called me back thirty minutes later.

I had hoped for a male doctor, so we could handle this man-to-man, but as I stepped behind the curtained room and saw a young female nurse waiting for me, all my hopes went up in smoke. Rick followed me inside the small room and positioned himself in the corner to observe. I was convinced he was here for the sole purpose of having a good laugh.

The nurse glanced at me, her eyes widened and her breathing hitched. She looked young, too young to be a nurse, and was pretty in an innocent, sweet way that I didn't normally go for.

'Hello. Caden Ellis?' she asked. Her voice was soft and laced with concern.

It took me a second to respond. 'Cade.'

'Please have a seat.' She gestured to the white-paper-covered exam table and began flipping through my chart. 'My name's Alexa. I'm a nursing student and I'll be assisting the doctor tonight. Do you mind if I ask you a few simple questions before we move on to the hard stuff?' Her eyes shifted nervously to my lap, and I couldn't help but grin.

'Sure.'

She nodded astutely. 'Fine, then. Let's begin.' She sat down on the rolling stool beside me and wheeled herself closer. 'Your weight?'

'Two-ten.'

'Height?'

'Six-one.'

She scribbled it down on her file. 'And your age?'

'Twenty-two.'

She bit back a smile, though I didn't really know why.

Her hair was somewhere between blonde and brown, and she had large blue eyes that matched the color of a crystal-clear sky.

She was petite yet shapely, nicely filling out her blue hospital scrubs with curves in all the right places. She had a full rosebud mouth and a small upturned nose, and even in her work uniform she looked polished and put together – giving the impression she'd been raised to be poised and proper. A far cry from how I grew up.

She finished the forms and busied herself with the medical equipment to check my vitals. Even though her presence was professional, it did nothing to help weaken my erection. In fact, I think my damn cock became even harder just to taunt me.

She placed a stethoscope over my heart and listened for several moments before jotting down a few notes. I watched her work, a smile tugging on my lips.

'So, Cade.' She smiled up at me with straight, white teeth while she attached a blood-pressure cuff to my bicep. 'What seems to be the problem?'

Fuck. She was going to make me say it. 'It's there…' I tapped the clipboard she held. 'On the forms I filled out in the waiting room…'

She looked down, a frown tugging at her mouth. 'Yes. I see that. But if you could just please explain… um, how this happened. Is this the first time, you've, um…experienced this?'

'I've never taken performance-enhancing drugs before if that's what you're asking.' The words from the overplayed commercial rang through my head. *'If you have an erection lasting longer than four hours, seek immediate medical help.'*

I tore my eyes from the thin fabric stretched taut across her chest, but not before she caught me looking. She looked down at her chest to see what I was staring at and frowned. She pulled an oversized Q-tip I hadn't even noticed from the pocket over her breast. 'Don't worry, I won't be using this on you.'

That wasn't what had captured my attention, but I was relieved all the same at not being caught ogling her breasts. I felt like a real asshole, sitting here sporting wood and staring at the nurse's tits. *Classy.* It was as if my dick thought we were here to pick up a willing participant to ease his discomfort. *Sadly, no, little man.* I felt his pain. I cleared my throat and looked down.

Alexa worked quickly and methodically, pumping up the arm cuff and pressing her fingers into my wrist to get my pulse while she studied the ticking hands on her wristwatch. I took the opportunity to study her more closely, noticing the way her face held absolute concentration as she worked. She was trying her damnedest not to be distracted by me. It wasn't the usual effect I had on females.

'So can you tell me more about when this problem began?' She glanced down at my forms, which I'd deliberately left vague, jotting down only the most critical issues—name, medical insurance, and oh, yeah, a painful erection. I'd been hoping to speak with a male doctor who'd seen this kind of thing before, not an attractive young nurse, dammit.

I hesitated and Rick laughed. 'We were beginning our film shoot and my star here got stage fright. I gave him a couple of the little blue pills I keep on hand just in case.'

Her mouth pursed into a pouty frown again as she looked from Rick back to me. I glanced down, motioning to the tense erection straining against my jeans.

'Oh, my.' Her hand flew to her mouth and she involuntarily took a step back.

Her response was so honest, so damn innocent, I almost chuckled. Almost. But the majority of my blood supply was sitting south at the moment, which delayed any normal responses.

'So, wait…what business are you guys in?'

'Adult entertainment,' Rick and I answered at the exact same moment.

'You mean…porn?' Alexa asked.

I winced.

4

Rick reached across to hand Alexa a business card. 'Mrs. X Entertainment,' he said proudly.

I didn't explain that it was the romantic, softer stuff, and that the film company had won awards for being female-friendly—the features that had attracted me to working with them in the first place. Because frankly, none of that mattered. It was porn, and that was all she was going to see. She probably figured I was some sort of player or a sex addict. I saw it in her eyes, and there was no use fighting it. It wasn't like I would ever see this girl again. She would never know about the little girl in my custody, and the mortgage, groceries, and utilities I was responsible for.

After taking a moment to compose herself the nurse jumped into action, grabbing a white paper gown and thrusting it towards me. 'Here. Get undressed and put this on so that it opens in the front and I'll be right back.' She fled the room without another word.

A few days ago when I'd signed on for the whole adult entertainment thing it'd been easy. I showed up and posed for some modeling photos for the website. Wearing just boxers I lounged on a bed with a beautiful girl named Desiree. They had us pose in various positions that grew increasingly intimate—me licking her neck, her nipples, and then her clit. It wasn't sexual, like you'd think it would be. We had to hold still and hold each pose for several seconds while the camera clicked away, so it wasn't like I was actually getting her off. I just sort of held my tongue against her. It was…different. And when they'd asked me to shed the boxers, I wasn't hard yet. Without a word, Desiree—like the pro she was—reached down and rubbed her long, manicured fingers over my package until I was erect. After that I spent another hour posing with her. Modeling was the easy part. It was the filming that would prove to be difficult.

*

Three Hours Earlier

Rick sauntered over to give me a pep talk. 'You ready for this?'

I took a deep breath and glanced at the staged set—a white leather couch set against floor-to-ceiling windows in the chic loft the studio had rented. It all felt cold and contrived, but what did I expect? It was just sex. I could do this. It was the one thing I knew for sure I was good at. And most importantly, it paid a lot—enough for me to afford Lily's medical care.

I pictured her sweet face peeking out over the edge of her quilt when I'd tucked her in earlier tonight. I'd told her Becca was going to babysit and she wouldn't see me until morning. She'd tightened her lips and nodded. She didn't like the dark, and sometimes even preferred to crawl into my bed at night, but she was putting on her brave face.

'Cade?' Rick asked, pulling my attention back to him.

'Yeah, I'll be fine.'

'That's my boy. Our actress should be here soon. She's a new girl. You'll love her. Young, sweet...' He made a sucking sound with his lips and his eyes got a faraway look to them. I shuddered. Throwing aside the fact that he was an adult-film director, Rick's demeanor just screamed sleazy.

I was almost starting to regret my decision to work for him, but visions of dollar signs kept floating before my eyes. Rick had seen me in the boxing ring several times over the previous year, and a few months ago had begun approaching me after matches, promising big money if I was ever interested in working for him. At the time, I laughed it off. But the fights brought in less than steady money and as things got worse with Lily I bit the bullet and decided to give it a shot.

The makeup artist approached, thankfully distracting Rick from whatever perverted thoughts were currently running through his head. I removed my robe at her request and she began airbrushing some type of bronzing spray over my shoulders and chest. I didn't like the smell of it, but I pushed it from my mind and focused on what I had to do.

'So the biggest thing for you to remember is *control*. No money shots until I say so. So if you need to slow down, or switch positions, just go ahead and do it. As long as you don't come until I give the signal. We need plenty of shots and positions before that can happen,' Rick reminded me.

'Got it. Shouldn't be a problem.'

He laughed. 'Confident. I like that.'

Confidence usually wasn't a problem for me, but I couldn't deny there was a hint of performance anxiety at the thought of having sex with a girl I'd never met, on camera, in front of a roomful of people—lighting techs, director, film crew, and a few others whose roles I didn't know. I tried not to focus on all that and instead reminded myself about the money Rick had promised me.

'What about her? Shouldn't I talk to her first? Find out what she likes, how she gets off?'

Rick laughed, and slapped my shoulder. 'Silly boy. This is a porn shoot, not a first date. She'll fake it, so don't worry about her having an orgasm. Just focus on you.'

I could only imagine what a conversation like that with a stranger might sound like…. *So do you like penetration or clitoral stimulation to have an orgasm?* God, was I an idiot or what? I was overthinking this shit.

The front door opened and everyone turned. 'And there she is! Beautiful girl…' Rick headed over to greet the wide-eyed starlet entering the apartment.

I couldn't help but notice how scared she looked. And young. Holy shit, was this girl even eighteen? I watched as Rick helped her out of her jacket and steered her by the shoulders over to the makeup chair.

*

When Alexa returned I was seated on the exam table, the paper gown loosely closed around me. Rick hadn't offered to leave while I changed. He and a whole room full of people had already seen me buck-naked though, so I figured it didn't matter much at this point. This whole night just needed to fucking end.

Alexa washed her hands and carefully arranged an ice pack over my groin. I shifted and let out a grunt at the surprise of the coldness, and Alexa's eyes flicked up to mine. 'Is it okay?' she asked, softly.

'Fine,' I muttered and bit back the string of curse words I wanted to let rip and adjusted the ice pack so it wasn't sitting directly on my nuts.

Rick leaned against the exam table and chuckled to himself as if he found our interaction amusing. It was clear I was intrigued by her and the way her eyes wandered the room, desperate to look anywhere but directly at me, or rather at my swollen appendage, she was clearly uncomfortable.

'You can see why we hired him, huh, sweetheart?' Rick grinned proudly and elbowed her softly in the side.

Her cheeks flushed pink and she tucked her chin to her chest.

'Let's just get on with it,' I growled. I didn't care about the exam or being exposed, I just wanted to end her embarrassment as quickly as possible.

I didn't know why I'd listened to Rick and taken those damn pills. I was attracted to the model he'd hired, that wasn't the problem. She was very pretty, petite and trim, but she'd looked fucking terrified. I'd tried to make polite conversation before the shoot began, but even small talk was too much for her. She excused herself to the kitchen, where she sat perched on a bar stool, her eyes closed tight, chest rising and falling as she took deep breaths.

After she finally talked herself into going through with it, I was so weirded out that I couldn't even keep my erection up—something that had never been a problem for me before.

I wasn't about to fuck some girl who was terrified of me. Sorry, not a turn-on. Rick had assumed it was a performance issue, and stupidly I'd accepted the pills from him rather than explaining why I didn't want to go through with it. Eventually I had to man up and explain the situation to him, but not before the damage was done.

'So, you're a porn star?' Alexa asked, her eyes flicking up to mine briefly before darting away again.

She was as nervous as a field mouse in a stampede. 'Does that bother you?' I bluffed. She didn't need to know that this was my first ever film and I hadn't even followed through. Besides, she'd already judged me. No sense in trying to defend my honor.

Her eyes met mine again and held. 'No.' Her voice sounded sure, but I couldn't help noticing the blush creeping up her neck to color her cheeks. I wouldn't be all that surprised to learn she was a virgin, with how self-conscious and unsure of herself she was. All the more reason to stay the hell away from her.

Watching her work, her small hands moving about to care for me stirred something inside. It'd been a long time since someone had taken care of me.

The doctor strode into the room—male, late-forties, and strait-laced, which put me at ease.

After covering the basics—that I'd taken two of little blue pills even though only *one* was recommended and yes, I'd been fully erect going on four and half hours now—the doctor, thankfully, got right down to business, opening my robe. The swollen appendage jutted out in front of me, proudly saluting the doctor and Alexa.

'There he is!' Rick beamed proudly. This dude was twisted. Why the hell was he so interested in my cock? Sure it was above average, I knew that much. After Rick had approached me about starring in one of his movies, I'd looked up the statistics online and measured myself, just out of curiosity. It was much larger than average according to what I'd read online. But still, his interest was creepy. I reminded myself that he dealt with the human body all day long and that he was just thinking about the money I could make him when he looked at it, but that didn't mean I liked another man eyeing my dick with such enthusiasm.

My eyes flicked up to watch Alexa's expression. Bad fucking idea. Her mouth had dropped open, and her chest was heaving with shallow breaths. I practically felt her gaze caressing me.

'Is he family?' the doctor asked, gingerly inspecting me.

'Nope.'

The doctor tipped his head to the door, motioning to Rick. 'Would you mind stepping out of the room, sir?'

'Sure thing, Doc.' Rick nodded. 'I'm out of here just as soon as you tell me there'll be no permanent damage to the money maker.'

The doctor looked up at him, not amused. 'He'll live. Now please go.'

Apparently satisfied by the doctor's answer, Rick gave me a wink, patted my shoulder and exited the room.

'So how exactly do you treat this?' I was almost afraid to ask.

Alexa's eyes shifted to the floor, like she knew I wasn't going to like the answer. Not good.

'I'm going to give you a dose of medicine—a combination of a steroid and a muscle relaxant to see if that will return things to normal. You'll take these orally and we'll wait about thirty minutes. If that doesn't work, I may have to insert a thin needle into the shaft and extract blood manually.' The doctor made a few notes in my file and left the room.

I swallowed down a lump in my throat. The fucking pills had to work. I wouldn't be able to handle him bringing a needle anywhere near my dick without punching the poor guy in the face.

10

Alexa returned a few minutes later with a tiny plastic cup containing two pills and a cup of water for me. I downed the pills and water in a single gulp. Once again, she arranged the ice pack on my lap, her hand brushing against my dick, which made it jump. I saw her bite her lip to avoid smiling.

'Thanks,' I muttered, passing the cup back to her.

'You're welcome. Sit tight and I'll be back to check your progress in a little while.'

I'd never been so happy to go soft in my entire life, but twenty minutes later my erection slackened and I hopped down from the exam table and began dressing. Just as I was pulling on my jeans, Alexa came back to check on me.

The look of surprise on her face stopped me short.

'I think I'm good to go,' I explained.

Her eyes travelled down the length of my body, stopping once they reached the no-longer-straining bulge in my jeans. 'Oh.'

'Thanks for everything.' I grabbed my jacket from the chair, and started past her. Her hands darted out and pressed against my chest. 'You can't just leave. Dr. Chancellor wanted to um… talk with you, about your, um, lifestyle. And see if we could offer STD testing.'

I laughed. 'Thanks anyway, but I'm good.' I barely had time to date, let alone have sex, but when I did I always used a condom. Not to mention that Rick insisted I get tested as an agreement to work for him. All I wanted to do now was get home, check on Lily, and forget this whole night ever happened. 'Okay. Be safe,' she said, and stepped out of the way as I fled past her, ready to put the whole experience behind me.

11

Chapter 2

Alexa

When I woke and fumbled for my cell phone to check the time, I was shocked to discover it was already four in the afternoon. I stretched and flung back my duvet, sighing because despite the late hour, my body was *so* not ready to leave my heavenly soft pillowtop.

Working the midnight shift was wreaking havoc with my system. Each night I worked the late shift, I woke later and later in the afternoon. At least I had tonight off—it was my twenty-first birthday, and I was going out with friends later. I could only imagine what MacKenzie had planned. That girl, though I considered her my best friend in nursing school, was trouble with a capital T.

I sat down at my vanity and brushed out my hair. The bags under my eyes needed attention too, so I dotted on some eye cream before securing my hair back in a ponytail.

My parents didn't understand why I worked so hard. Money certainly wasn't the motivator—my family had more than we'd ever spend in a lifetime—but I wanted something more for myself. Something I was good at and kept me busy. Their only goal for me was to meet a wealthy, well-bred man and become some sort of Stepford Wife, a desire we did not share. A life like that sounded incredibly boring to me. And if my mother's afternoon

12

combination of happy pills and wine-spritzers were any indication, it was a life spent unfulfilled. No thanks.

Once in the kitchen, I slid a coffee pod into the one-cup maker, the most used appliance in my kitchen since I rarely bothered to cook for one. I couldn't help but think back to the previous night, or more specifically, about Cade. Well, I was actually thinking of a certain part of his anatomy more than I was anything else, and giggled to myself. I'd seen a lot of strange things working the midnight shift in the emergency room, but that was one of the more memorable.

He was undeniably attractive, and that was even before I saw the python he was packing in his pants. He was tall and ridiculously toned from head to toe, with a rugged face and strong jaw line. His nose had a slight ridge that indicated it had probably been broken at some point, and those rich chocolate eyes of his had been surrounded by thick, dark lashes.

He'd had the strangest effect on me. I'd never been attracted to a patient. Ever. It was my job, and I rarely noticed details about the actual person. That statement sounded harsh, but I saw the people who came in and out of the hospital as clinical objects. I only noticed the details I needed to do my job—like where there best vein line was to start an IV or draw blood, or calculating meds based on weight—standard things like that. But with him, I couldn't focus on what I needed to. Instead, I noticed how his dark eyes followed my every movement, the thickness of the vein running up the length of his shaft, and the tension in his body at his obvious discomfort. I also noticed the tattoo peeking out from the collar of his T-shirt as if crawling up his neck. I wanted to see the rest of it, even if the mere thought of that made my tummy erupt in nerves. And I knew he could tell how frazzled I was with that annoying amused smirk tugging at his lips.

*

When the doorbell chimed, I jogged to the intercom panel to buzz in MacKenzie and Tyson. I opened my apartment door and found MacKenzie marching up the stairs, a brown paper sack filled with liquor bottles in one hand and a plastic container in the other. Tyson was carrying a bouquet of pink roses. Tyson was like a brother to me, but I wasn't sure we were always on the same page.

I'd made Kenzie promise me no big party, just the three of us going out and enjoying a few cocktails, and so far it appeared she'd kept her end of the bargain.

'Our baby girl's growing up, Ty!' MacKenzie squealed and pulled me in for a hug. I patted her back and pulled away for some personal space. I wasn't the best hugger in the world. Tyson laughed and navigated around us, entering my apartment. He knew better than to try and hug me after I went completely stiff in his arms the one and only time he'd attempted it.

'Thanks for the roses,' I called to his back as he made his way into my kitchen to fetch a vase. He'd spent enough time in my apartment to know where everything was. Heck, I think he knew my apartment better than I did. Once I called him to ask how to clean my hair out of the clogged shower drain and he informed me I had a bottle of drain cleaner under the sink in the kitchen. He was good to me, and so was MacKenzie. She often forced me out of my shell, which, however painful at times, was good for me too.

MacKenzie took over the kitchen island, extracting various bottles of alcohol and mixers from her bag. Ty got the glasses and filled them with ice, while I stood and watched.

'What's in here?' I poked at the lid of the shallow plastic pan, expecting it to hold a cake.

'Jell-O shots,' MacKenzie answered, smiling. 'Try one.'

I pulled off the lid and set it aside. The pan was filled with small plastic shot glasses that contained a rainbow of jellied concoctions.

They certainly looked inviting. I selected a green one and tipped it up to my mouth, but the gelatinous mass remained firmly planted inside the cup.

MacKenzie laughed and glanced at Tyson. 'Teach her how, Ty. I forgot we had a Jell-O-shot virgin on our hands.' She measured two shots of clear liquor and dumped them over a glass full of ice, mixing the drink like it was second nature.

Ty smiled and rounded the island to stand next to me. 'Stick out your tongue.'

I narrowed my eyes at him.

He chuckled. 'Just do it.'

I complied and he brought the cup to my mouth, showing me how to swirl my tongue around the edge of it to loosen the Jell-O until it slipped out of the cup and into my mouth.

'Mmm. Green Apple?' I asked.

Ty wiped away a smear of Jell-O from my bottom lip and licked it from his finger.

MacKenzie nodded. 'Yep. And here's your birthday drink.'

It was pink and bubbly. I took a sip and found it surprisingly refreshing. You could hardly taste the vodka shots I'd seen her dump in. It was grapefruity and delish. 'Thanks.'

Once we all had drinks, courtesy of MacKenzie, Ty grabbed the pan of Jell-O shots and we made our way into the living room to sit in the center of my cream-colored shaggy rug.

'We need music.' MacKenzie opened my laptop and my heart nearly stopped. I leapt from my seat in an effort to stop her from seeing what she was about to see, but I was too late.

'Holy shit!'

My cheeks flamed as I remembered what I'd last used the computer for—I'd typed in the address for the porn website from the business card when I got home and searched until I found Cade's pictures.

15

'What is it?' Ty asked, peeking around MacKenzie's His face scrunched in disgust. 'Gah!' He jumped back from the computer like he'd just been stung.

'You look at porn, Alexa?' The surprise in MacKenzie's voice was unmistakable. 'I'm not judging, not at all, proud is more like it—I'm just surprised. You've always seemed sort of innocent.'

I swallowed and grabbed the laptop from her lap, pulling it onto my own. 'It's not what you think.' I opened my music library and started my playlist of indie-rock, then set the computer aside.

MacKenzie laughed, throwing her head back. 'Sorry, sweetheart, but that's gonna require an explanation. I mean, you've never taken a Jell-O shot, you were raised by the Waltons, your freaking panty-drawer is organized by color and day of the week. Spill it, babe.'

Tyson glanced up from his drink. 'You've got day-of-the-week underwear? Oh, I've gotta see this.' He stood and wandered down the hall into my bedroom. MacKenzie and I jumped to our feet to follow.

'Ty!' I called. 'Get out of there!'

He chuckled and pulled open the top drawer of my hand-carved, pale-pink dresser. 'Holy shit, you weren't kidding, Kenz.' He lifted a pair of white cotton briefs from the top of the pile and held them up to inspect. 'Sunday,' he read the backside, chuckling.

I snatched them from his grasp, tossed them back in the drawer and slammed it shut with my hip. 'Enough. Out.' I shooed them from my bedroom. Yes, I bought the packaged cotton undies. They were comfy. Sue me.

MacKenzie stood her ground, blocking the door to my bedroom. 'Only if you tell us the story of you looking at porn. I bet you don't even own a sex toy do you?'

'I'll tell you.' I navigated my way around her out into the hallway. But I was *so* not answering the sex-toy question. Even if Ty was like a brother to us, he was still male, and I wasn't about to admit that I had a vibrator tucked in the back of my underwear drawer. God, I would have been mortified if they'd found that.

Once we were seated on the living room rug again I downed a few more Jell-O shots to ease my nerves and pulled a throw pillow into my lap. MacKenzie sat across from me, looking smug, leaning back against the sofa.

'Okay. So last night in the ER…' I grabbed another shot and slurped down the gelatinous mouthful, needing to fortify myself at the memory of Cade's erection.

'How big would you say it was?' MacKenzie asked once I was through my story, leaning forward with eager curiosity.

'Ah hell, I'm getting another drink,' Ty announced, standing to head into the kitchen.

After considering—and rejecting a nearby candlestick and finding nothing else adequate in my living room to showcase the full length of Cade's manhood, Kenzie and I made our way into the kitchen, giggling at my idea to retrieve a cucumber from the refrigerator.

I reached into the crisper drawer and modeled the large vegetable in front of my crotch. 'This looks about right.'

MacKenzie took my shoulders, turning me from side to side so I could model it at various angles. 'Damn. That boy is hung.'

Tyson retreated to the bathroom while MacKenzie and I made our way back into the living room. She hoisted the cucumber proudly over her head, waving it in time with the music, and led the way back to my computer.

MacKenzie settled onto the sofa, the laptop balanced on her knees and I scooted in beside her to…supervise.

'Click here,' I told her, pointing to the tab labeled Models. The title had seemed a little strange to me, but I supposed that sounded classier than saying porn stars. The pictures were mostly topless girls posing seductively. MacKenzie scrolled past the photos of the girls. Last night I'd thoroughly inspected each image, wondering if

Cade had slept with them, and which he preferred best. All of the girls were thin and tanned with large, fake breasts. I didn't want to, but my mind had inevitably made comparisons to my own body.

I was of average height, average weight. My breasts were decidedly real, they fell several inches when I removed my bra, and I had far too many freckles to be considered sexy. Pretty, maybe, but certainly not on par with the type of women he usually slept with. But all thoughts of insecurity vanished when I'd spotted Cade's photo.

'That's him.' I pointed at the photo.

It said his name was Sebastian, but it was definitely Cade. He was standing near a weight bench, gym shorts loose on his narrow hips to show his cut abs and he was smirking like he knew a secret the rest of us didn't.

'*Damn*. He's fucking hot.'

I giggled. 'I know.'

MacKenzie clicked on his photo. Though I had spent time last night poring over each one, I couldn't help but lean forward to join in her inspection. He had a full page of photos. In many of them he was wearing only a pair of black boxer briefs, and then a few where the boxers had been removed and all of him was proudly on display. The tattoo I'd wondered about was a tribal design that covered his left shoulder and crawled up his chest, ending at his neck.

I blushed at the sight of his fully erect cock and heat crept up my chest until I was rosy and warm. I couldn't help but reminisce about being near Cade in the semi-private hospital room, where I'd been close enough to feel the heat of his skin and smell of the scent of his musky arousal.

MacKenzie scrolled down to the bio beneath the photos. I'd read it last night, but couldn't resist reading it again over her shoulder. It said he was their newest model, and worked exclusively for their site. The bio claimed he was extremely professional to work with and always focused on making sure the girls felt comfortable. Outside of work he enjoyed working out and listening to rock music. It sounded like a clichéd line of bull, but that didn't keep me from grasping at every bit of information I could get.

Tyson appeared from the kitchen, this time with a bottle of beer, and sank down on the chair across the room.

'Ty, you want to see what a real man looks like?' MacKenzie teased.

I elbowed her side. Tyson was only a few inches taller than me, and had a slight build, but he was cute and I didn't like her tearing him down. Especially since he regularly caught flack for being one of only a few male nursing students.

'I get to see that every day, babe. I'm good.' He polished off the rest of his beer.

MacKenzie closed the laptop. 'Let's go out. If I look at any more of these, I'll bang the first guy I see at the club.'

By the time we arrived, the Jell-O shots had caught up with me. Tyson slipped his arm around my waist and helped me inside. Once we were stationed at the bar, he deposited me safely on a barstool, refused MacKenzie's request for more shots, and ordered me a beer and a water.

With our drinks in hand, we found a corner booth and slid into the seats.

I slumped back against the seat, resting my head against Ty's shoulder. 'What was in these Jell-O thingies? I feel funny.'

MacKenzie laughed. 'Vodka. I thought you knew Jell-O shots had booze in them.'

Ty grasped my chin, turning my face to his. 'How many of those did you have, Lex?'

I tried to count and lost track. 'Um, ten? Twelve?'

'Shit,' he said, and took the bottle of beer from my hand, replacing it with the water.

'Damn it, Kenzie. You said you'd watch out for her tonight.'

MacKenzie waved him off. 'She's drunk, not dead, Tyson. Calm down. It's her twenty-first birthday, and P.S.—you're not her dad.' She knocked back a healthy swig of her own drink.

'Don't fight, you guys. I'm fine.' I reached out to pat each of them reassuringly but fumbled. 'See?'

They both laughed at my lack of coordination.

'Sometimes I forget how sheltered you are, Alexa. I swear you act like you were raised by the Cleavers, with your day-of-the-week cotton underpants and everything.' she chuckled.

I sat up straighter in my seat. 'Just because I'm a virgin to Jell-O shots doesn't mean anything. Hell, I'm a virgin in every sense—' I slapped a hand over my mouth. Crap! I hadn't meant to say that out loud.

MacKenzie grabbed my shoulders. 'Are you serious right now?'

I nodded, reluctantly. Kenzie's and Tyson's faces were both filled with surprise at my revelation. 'What? It's not like I'm proud of it. I don't want to be this way anymore.'

MacKenzie took my hand. 'Babe, it's nothing to be ashamed of. But if you do want to get rid of it—it's not that difficult to do. Your parents did have the birds and bees talk with you, right?'

I grabbed my beer away from Ty and took a fortifying sip. 'I'm not like you. I couldn't have a one-night stand.'

'Well, don't come crying to me when you find yourself old and living alone with a bunch of cats.'

I took another pull from my bottle, not about to tell her I'd been thinking about getting a cat lately.

'Leave her alone, Kenzie,' Tyson said, removing the beer from my grasp yet again. He leaned over to me. 'If you want me to help you, just let me know.'

MacKenzie swatted Tyson's hand away from my thigh. 'No, Ty. I get to help pick him out. Sort of a birthday present.' She smiled.

I rolled my eyes, blowing off their suggestions. I was not picking out a random guy to sleep with on my twenty-first birthday. And I sure as hell wasn't sleeping with Tyson. Gah! Could you imagine? He's like a brother to me.

'Oh my God! Alexa, look.' MacKenzie pointed across the bar. 'It's the guy from the website.'

Chapter 3

Cade

I sat at the bar nursing a beer, lost in my thoughts.

'You want a nipple on that bottle, man? Stop being a little bitch and drink up,' Ian said, knocking back his own beer in a few swallows.

I shot him a warning look. 'Don't fuck with me tonight, I'm not in the mood.' I'd been hell-bent on getting drunk tonight, needing a few hours' peace from the worry that constantly followed me around, but somehow I was failing even at that. 'Lily's latest surgery bill came.'

'Sorry, man.' Ian tipped his beer, clinking the bottle against mine. 'Let me know if I can help.'

I nodded. I'd never ask him for help, and we both knew it, but still, just that he offered meant a lot. Ian and I had been friends since the eighth grade when I moved here to live with my grandparents. He knew all about my sister Lily, and the condition that left her poor little spine and legs tangled and twisted. After my parents' three-strikes-you're-out meth bust that landed them both in prison when she was three, and my grandparents each passing within a year after that, I'd had sole custody of her. She was six now and a sassy little thing that didn't know the meaning of the word disabled. It was one of the many things I loved about that

22

little girl. But her care wasn't cheap, which left me constantly worrying about money.

Ian, a lifelong martial-arts enthusiast, had introduced me to cage fighting a couple of years ago. It was a perfect fit. The opportunity to earn fast money and take out my pent-up aggression all at once. But it wasn't enough. And then my latest dumbass venture came along. Rick had approached both Ian and I, but I was the only one hard up enough for cash to consider it. Or the only one dumb enough, take your pick. Ian knew I was working for Rick, but didn't want any of the details, so of course I hadn't mentioned my late-night visit to the ER.

After getting the bill for Lily's latest surgery, I realized it wasn't just a well-paying job I needed, it was one that came with health insurance, too. But if I could stick it out and film even a couple of videos, I'd have more than enough to pay the bill. Then I could focus on cleaning up my act and getting a real job, for Lily's sake.

Realizing I was lost in my thoughts again, Ian cleared his throat. 'Stop stressing, bro. You get plenty of that during the week. We haven't been out in God knows how long, and since you have a babysitter for Lil tonight, we need to make good use of this time.'

'Yeah? And how do we do that?' Hitting the gym for a late workout session, followed by a hot shower and my bed sounded like a perfectly good use of my time. I didn't even think I was capable of catching a buzz at the moment.

'For starters, we need to make getting some pussy priority number one.'

I shook my head, not about to explain to him that tomorrow I'd be getting plenty of that on set. And with that bill hanging over my head, I sure as shit needed to perform this time.

Ian tipped his head toward a booth across the room. 'And I think you're in luck, bro. Those girls over there are staring at you.'

I turned from the bar, drawing my beer up to my lips as I scanned the room. With a jolt of surprise, I spotted the pretty little nurse from the other night, seated in a booth with a couple of friends.

What the hell?

The other woman at the table waved me over.

'Do you know them?' he asked.

'Yeah. Sorta.' I threw a few bills on the counter and told Ian I'd see him later. I sauntered over to where they sat.

'Hey there, sexy,' Alexa's friend said, trailing her fingers down my forearm. 'Saw your website. That shit was hot.'

My eyes flew to Alexa's. She'd told her friends about what I did? And what… Googled me? 'Alexa?'

She blushed and bit her bottom lip. 'Hi Cade.'

She wasn't even going to deny it? I supposed I had to get used to the fact that pictures of my cock were splashed all over the Internet, and that videos would soon follow. I had a film shoot tomorrow that I had to get through. I'd given Rick a piece of my mind about hiring girls that looked so young, and he promised he'd pair me with Mollie, an experienced pro I was sure to love, if I gave it another shot.

'Have a seat, Cade. Or is it Sebastian?' Alexa's friend asked. 'I'm MacKenzie by the way, and this is Tyson.' She motioned to the guy seated with them. He gave me a weak smile, looking just as uncomfortable as I was.

I remained standing. 'Call me Cade.'

Alexa's gaze travelled down the length of my chest and stomach, stopping just below my belt buckle. I couldn't help the smirk that tugged at my mouth, and she knew she had just been caught. She let out a huff of breath, folded her arms on the table and lay her head down to rest.

'Is she drunk?' I slid in next to her.

MacKenzie nodded, proudly. 'Yep. It's her twenty-first birthday.'

'Happy birthday.'

Alexa peeked one eye open and looked up at me. 'Thanks,' she grumbled before letting her eyes fall closed again.

'Perfect timing,' MacKenzie said, leaning forward on her elbows. 'We were just discussing Lex's birthday present.'

Alexa roused from her sleepy state and slapped a hand over MacKenzie's mouth. 'No, Kenz.'

MacKenzie dutifully removed Alexa's hand and squeezed it, before placing it on the table. 'Hush. You should be thanking me right now. You see, Alexa here is a virgin, and what better birthday present than to lose her virginity to someone skilled at giving female pleasure? I mean, you do this for a living.' She kicked up an eyebrow. 'Right?'

I pulled back a swig of my beer. Was she fucking kidding me? 'Well, yeah, I might know a thing or two about that...' I took another mouthful from my bottle to shut myself up. I mean, sure, nobody had ever complained before, but that didn't mean I was the hotshot porn star they saw on the website. Except they all *thought* I was. Hell.

Alexa looked up and met my gaze, her eyes wide with curiosity. *Christ*. She couldn't look at me like that, or I wasn't going to be able to hold it together.

Even though I believed it, I had a hard time understanding how she could still be a virgin on her twenty-first birthday. She was beautiful, pure and innocent. Her hair flowed in soft curls over her shoulders, resting just at the top of her full breasts. She was fucking perfection, and she didn't even know it. Her skin looked so soft, I wanted to reach across the table and stroke my thumb along her cheek just to prove to myself that it couldn't possibly be as soft as it looked. I settled instead for taking another drink. At this rate, I was going to need another beer really soon.

MacKenzie raised her glass in the air, as if to toast herself. 'Best idea ever!' She signaled the waitress and asked for a round of shots for the table. 'Patron okay?'

I nodded my indifference. Mostly I just wanted to know what Alexa was thinking right at that moment and what exactly she had told her friends about me.

The shots arrived and I took the glass from Alexa's fumbling fingertips. 'No more for you, cupcake.' I downed both my shot and hers, one after the other, the liquor burning on its way down.

She pouted, and took a sip of the water I pushed in front of her. But as we watched each other, her lips parted and her breaths grew faster. She leaned forward in interest, a shaky smile on her lips that grew bolder with each passing second. A bark of laughter from her friend Tyson surprised us all. 'Are you fucking kidding me? This guy? No. Alexa, if you're really going to do this, it should be me. Not some guy you don't even know, who probably has God-knows-what kind of diseases.'

Alexa swallowed visibly. As insane as this idea was, it was her decision. I forced my mouth shut, and kept my face composed. A low wave of nerves rolling through my stomach told me I wanted this—I wanted her—more than I had any right to.

'Okay,' she squeaked. 'Just let me think.' She pressed her fingers to her temples.

An unexpected surge of protectiveness sprung up inside me, and I found myself holding my breath.

MacKenzie shook her head. 'Lex, please, please, I beg of you, on behalf of women everywhere. Have hot, kinky sex with the porn star. Tyson will always be around.' She waved in his direction and he narrowed his eyes at her.

One thing was clear as day to me. Tyson had feelings for her. Real feelings. I should probably stop cock-blocking the poor bastard, but the look in Alexa's eyes told me she didn't return his feelings.

Not one bit. Her eyes wandered down my chest again and she bit her lip. Her cheeks flushed pink. She was growing turned on by just the thought of being with me. Fuck, I was going to get hard right here if she didn't stop looking at me like that.

Tyson set his drink down. 'Come on, Lex, this isn't you. You play things safe. You're not going to do…him' he tipped his head toward me 'and we all know it.'

She frowned and pulled her bottom lip into her mouth, considering his words. 'I'm sick of everyone thinking I'm Miss Goody Two-shoes, with my perfect grades, and days of the week panties. You know what? I have my Wednesdays on today—it's Saturday— and that's a pretty sad way of rebelling, huh?'

Days of the week? Damn, picturing her in her panties was doing nothing to tame my overactive libido.

'Well forget that! I'm doing this.' Alexa straightened her shoulders, which pushed her tits out. That little tank top she was wearing left very little to the imagination. And fuck it to hell, her nipples were hard. That protective surge I'd felt earlier was back, nagging at me more insistently. I would not stand back and let just anyone touch that pretty little pussy of hers. I'd kick Tyson's ass to keep him away from her if I had to. Which wouldn't be difficult, considering I was ready to knock his teeth in if he looked at her like that again.

'Lex?' Tyson asked, his voice soft and pleading.

Alexa's eyes were back on mine, drinking me in. She just sat there blinking up at me, waiting expectantly. *Oh fuck, I was going to hell.*

'Fuck it, I'll do it myself,' I growled.

Her swift intake of breath at my declaration made the hair on the back of my neck stand. I swallowed roughly. 'But not tonight. You've had too much to drink.'

Her mouth dropped open in surprise.

'Do you have a pen?' I motioned to MacKenzie's giant purse sitting on the table. She jumped into action, rooting around inside and seconds later, thrust a pen toward me. I reached across the table and turned over Alexa's arm, brushing the soft flesh with my thumb. Her skin *was* as soft as I'd imagined, and the sensation stopped me in my tracks for a second. 'If you still want to tomorrow, and I doubt you will, sweetheart, meet me here.' I scribbled the address along her inner arm, tossed some bills on the table and left.

Chapter 4

Alexa

'Alexa.' My mother's disapproving tone demanded my attention. She tapped a red lacquered nail against the table. 'You look a mess. I hope your night out with your friends was worth it.'

I straightened the sundress around my knees, and shifted in my seat. Though my memories of the night before were somewhat foggy, a slow smile crossed my lips. It was everything a twenty-first birthday was supposed to be. And this morning, I'd had the hangover from hell to prove it.

She dug through her purse, offering me a compact. 'You need some concealer.' The only thing my mother criticized more than my poor manners were my looks, and though applying makeup in public would have typically earned me an exasperated sigh, apparently things were dreadful enough that immediate intervention was warranted. That and I guess being tucked back in the tall booth of a dim restaurant wasn't exactly public.

I took her compact and flipped it open, inspecting my appearance. There were dark circles under my eyes, and my hair hung limply around my face since I hadn't had time this morning to dry it. I twisted it into a low, loose bun and secured it with a few pins dug from the bottom of my purse. Then I swiped some of the concealer under my eyes until I was satisfied it was the best I could do.

29

'That's better,' my mother said, holding out her hand to retrieve the compact.

We were waiting for my father to arrive, and so far he was an entire seven minutes late. I was sure he'd get an earful about it later. My mother had chosen the restaurant –a high-end steak-house. I was never much of a meat eater, but she and my dad were on a high-protein diet. I scanned the menu for something that didn't make me want to hurl. I decided on a Caesar salad with grilled shrimp.

My father arrived, slipping into the booth beside my mother and offering her a chaste peck on the cheek in apology. 'Sorry I'm late. Business meeting ran over.' He reached across the table and gave my hand a squeeze.

I nodded. 'It's okay, Daddy.'

I knew my dad had a stressful job. He was a partner at an accounting firm and worked hard to give me and my mother everything and then some. I couldn't be mad at him for being a few minutes late to a lunch I didn't want to be at either.

My stomach was still queasy from last night, and I nibbled on bread and sipped my water while my parents discussed the upgrades they had planned to our vacation home in Aspen. My mind wandered to last night's events. Oh, all right, directly back to Cade. This morning while I'd stood under the steaming hot spray of the shower, scrubbing his address from my forearm, I couldn't help but remember his sexy, challenging smile.

Seriously, who in the hell arranges a meeting to lose their virginity? It wasn't like I was actually going to go through with having sex with a porn star, and a complete stranger at that. God, was that insane or what? I really needed to keep MacKenzie on a tighter leash. This was all her doing. When I remembered the look she gave me when I admitted that I was a virgin, I shuddered. Even Tyson had jumped in, saying he'd be happy to make me a woman himself. Too bad there was zero attraction there. He was a nice guy, and I knew he'd do anything for me—but that? No thanks. It'd be like kissing my brother. *Gross.*

The look on Cade's face at hearing Ty step up to the plate was pure anger, and when his eyes flashed to mine they were filled with something else... Longing? No. I couldn't think about the possibility of desire in Cade's expression. That had me shuddering for an entirely different reason.

But what was etched most deeply into my memory was the smug look on his face, the certainty that I wouldn't have the guts to show up today.

That, coupled with my mother's disapproving glances and not-so-subtle hints about setting me up with Peter Wyndham III were enough to convince me. Even though I'd scrubbed away every trace of his writing from my skin, I remembered the address. *715 Evergreen Terrace.*

Not that I was actually going to go. God, could you imagine? *Sorry, Mom and Dad, I have to cut this horrendous lunch short to go meet a porn star so I can lose my virginity.* Ha! I choked on my water at the absurdity.

The few bites of solid food in my stomach and multiple glasses of iced water had returned me to my former self. I would go to Cade—but only to tell him off. Who the hell did he think he was? Offering his services like it was a total inconvenience for him, but still agreeing to take my virginity? I shuddered. He was about to get an earful.

My parents insisted on dessert, since it was my birthday after all, so I forced down several bites of cheesecake before saying goodbye to my parents. Once they were gone, I made my way to the restroom inside the restaurant and scanned my appearance in the full-length mirror. I adjusted the spaghetti straps of the form-fitting, cream-colored sundress and smoothed the fabric over my hips. Everything about my look, from the coral gloss on my lips to my French-pedicured feet encased in gold designer sandals ensured Cade would understand I was way out of his league. Satisfied I looked as good as I could manage on a hangover I straightened my shoulders and grabbed my handbag. This had nothing to do with seeing Cade again, and everything to do with letting him see what he'd never have.

When I pulled up in front of 715 Evergreen Terrace, I figured there had to be some sort of mistake. He'd probably given me a fake address, since I doubted Cade, the porn-star hottie lived in this suburban, middle-class neighborhood.

I put my car into park and switched off the engine. The house itself was small, but neat and tidy, its white siding freshly painted. A row of trimmed hedges bordered the small yard.

A black pick-up truck was parked in the driveway, but other than that, there was no telling if anyone was home. I checked my appearance in the rearview mirror one last time, took a deep breath and left the safety of my car before I chickened out completely.

I didn't get very far. A school bus had stopped on the corner, letting off a small army of children. The noisy kids scattered in different directions, parading home along the streets and sidewalks, but my attention was momentarily captured by a bright-eyed little girl, smaller than all the rest, who hobbled her way past me with the help of a tiny walker. She spared me a curious glance, but continued on, her eyes shining with determination.

'Caden!' she called, struggling to make her legs carry her in the direction of the house, where Cade had appeared on the front lawn. He crossed the last few feet separating them and lifted her easily from the ground, the walker momentarily left aside.

'How was school, baby girl?' He planted a kiss in her blonde curls before lowering her to the ground.

'It was good. I colored a picture of a butterfly for you today.'

'Yeah? That sounds real nice. Is it in your backpack?'

She nodded, her curls bouncing as she did so. The pink backpack was nearly as big as she was. I thought maybe he'd take the bag from her shoulders, or help her up the ramp that led up to the porch, but he just looked on proudly as her little figure slowly shuffled upward, pushing the walker out in front of her with each step.

The little girl had captured Cade's complete attention and he'd yet to even notice me.

'Cade?' My voice sounded shaky and uneven even to my own ears.

He spun around and looked at me, still waiting by my car at the curb. 'Alexa?' Confusion etched into his features, creasing his brow.

Shit. I *so* should not have come. All my earlier venom about wanting to tell him off had evaporated at watching him with the little girl.

I watched as he connected the dots in his head, and the surprised expression on his face disappeared, a slow smile curving his lips. 'So you really want to go through with it, do you?'

And the venom was back. I marched across the yard, stopping just in front of him, and jabbed my finger into his chest. 'I'm not here to have sex with you, you sleazebag. You didn't think I'd show, so I only came here to prove you wrong.'

The front door opened and the little girl peeked out. 'Caden?' Her voice was full of questions and her eyes widened at the sight of me so close to Cade. I dropped my hand from his chest and stepped back. It was hard to be mad at him when such a sweet little girl obviously adored him.

'It's okay, Lily. Go on back in the house. I'll be in to help you with your stretches in just a minute.'

She scratched her belly and sighed. 'Can you make me a peanut butter and jelly?'

He chuckled. 'Sure will. Go turn on your 'toons for a minute.'

'M'kay!' she called happily, closing the door behind her as she disappeared inside.

'Is she…yours?'

He ran a hand across his hair and blew out a frustrated breath. 'Lily's my sister, but I have full custody. I have since she was three.'

'Oh.' He was raising his little sister? I took a step back at the weight of this new information. The strong bond between them was undeniable. 'Is it scoliosis?' I asked softly.

'Spina bifida,' he said, his eyes far away.

'Oh,' I said again. I knew it was a crippling childhood disease that left the spine twisted and often affected the legs, but not much else. 'I'm sorry.'

'We manage,' he bit out.

'I can see that. Look, I'm sorry. Why don't we just forget I ever came here?' I wanted to take another step back, to disappear entirely, but I remained where I was, fighting the urge to run.

'Why did you come here?' His gaze sparked with curiosity, the challenge in his tone unmistakable.

His eyes raked over my skin, and sent a brief chill skittering down my spine. I cursed myself for wearing this damn sundress and for how much skin was showing. My breasts pressed against the thin cotton fabric, reminding me this dress didn't accommodate for a bra and left me feeling a little too on display. I hated how his mere presence left me off balance and reeling.

'At least a little part of you was curious. You wouldn't have shown up otherwise.' He touched my shoulder, his thumb brushing along the exposed flesh next to the strap of my dress.

My eyes shut briefly at the intensity in his caress, and I uselessly opened and closed my mouth, unable to respond. Heck yeah, I was curious. I was curious what his stubble-covered jaw would feel like against my skin and what his full mouth would feel like covering mine.

He dropped his hand, seemingly unaware of the panty-melting effect he was having on me. 'Just so you know, I wasn't trying to embarrass you, or take advantage. I was trying to preserve some of your dignity. Your one friend was practically auctioning you off, and your other friend was ready to whip out his dick and take you right there. You should be thanking me.'

Thanking him? Yeah, right. But I guess it had put him in an awkward situation, too. 'Well, I only came here to tell you never mind. That I wasn't interested.'

'Really? That's why you drove all the way over here?' One of his eyebrows quirked upward in disbelief.

My cheeks reddened. I supposed curiosity had more than a little to do with it… Well, that, and I'd have done just about anything to get away from my mother's afternoon shopping plans for us.

'We both know there's more to it than that. A small part of you wants this, but I can be patient. I've got all the time in the world.'

He was right that I did want it, but I wasn't about to tell him that. His cockiness was now really beginning to get on my nerves. 'Get over yourself. It'll be a cold day in hell when I come asking you for sex.'

He laughed at my sudden outburst, the sound full and throaty. 'Whatever you say, cupcake.' He glanced back at the house where I knew his sister was waiting for him.

Hearing him mention about helping her with her stretches sent my mind tumbling in the direction of nursing school, and trying to remember what I knew about issues with the spine. 'Does she go to physical therapy?'

'Not anymore. I couldn't afford to keep it up, so I had the therapist teach me the exercises I could do with her at home.'

'Oh.' I seemed to keep saying that, increasingly finding myself at a loss for words. Over the past few minutes he'd transformed from an ultra-sexy, bad-for-you porn star into a loving, caring human being. He clearly loved his sister and worried over her condition. I didn't know what to do with this new information. 'I have to go. Besides, you have a PB and J to make.' I held my face impassive, trying like hell not to let him see just how confused I was becoming.

'Yeah, okay.' He stuffed his hands into his pockets, his forearms flexing with movement, a smug smile still on his lips.

I turned and headed for my car, his chuckle grating over my skin for what I assumed was the last time. How wrong I was.

Chapter 5

Cade

I stalked inside to find Lily planted in front of the TV, happily watching her 'toons. I headed back to the kitchen to fix her snack. As I smeared peanut butter on the bread, I shook my head in disbelief over the realization that Alexa had actually shown up. And I strongly doubted it was to tell me off, like she'd implied. I could read the curiosity on her face as clear as day.

I could also tell she was too prim and proper to let herself act on her unbidden desires. I knew her type—diamond-studded earrings, an expensive watch, and too-high expectations. Girls like that didn't go for guys like me. No, they wanted some douche bag named Scott who was well-mannered and sat behind a desk all day, doing fuck knows what, but pulling in a nice fat paycheck every week.

She had the face of an angel. I hadn't been able to resist brushing my fingers past her skin to see if she felt as soft as she looked. And when her eyes fluttered closed at my touch, my cock jerked in my jeans. I was twenty-two, not fifteen, but damn if my dick knew it.

'Mollie's here. You're going to fucking love her,' Rick assured me.

A tall, thin girl entered the room. She was built for sin, dressed in a black garter belt, stockings, black lace bra and sky-high heels. Long red hair cascaded over her shoulders and down her back.

'Sebastian?' she asked as she approached.

'Nice to meet you.' I offered her my hand. I couldn't believe I was actually going through with it. But I had to—for my own stubborn male pride, not to mention the money.

She looked wryly at my proffered hand and stepped in closer, separating any distance between us and patted my naked chest. 'Oh, you are fucking gorgeous, honey. This is going to be fun.'

I chuckled as a wave of shyness crested through me. I didn't even know this girl's real name—assuming it wasn't Mollie—and I was about to fuck her. But I figured it wasn't much different than the few times I'd taken girls home from the bar without even knowing their last names. Maybe it felt different because I was sober. Oh, and because there was a room full of people watching us.

'Rick told me it's your first time on film. Don't worry about trying too hard. Just have fun. And I won't get off with all these people watching me, so don't worry about that. It'll still feel good to me, so just do your thing. Okay?'

I nodded. 'You got it.' I liked her already. From what I'd seen, she was going to be easy to work with.

Rick's production company prided itself on exploring the intimate side of sex, rather than being typical hard-core porn. In this scene, we were lovers who'd been separated for a long time. I was arriving home from a business trip to find her waiting for me in lingerie. I was now dressed in dress slacks, a shirt and tie to complete the scene. We began at the front door, where the film crew captured a few initial scenes of us kissing.

Once we'd filmed that brief scene, we moved to the bedroom, with full-on lights and sound crew. Cameras were stationed around the room, all pointing directly at the bed.

Rick busied himself with the crew making sure everything was set the way he wanted it and then came back to stand in front of me and Mollie. 'We're set to start rolling, so you two going ahead and get started when you're ready. We're just here to capture your lovemaking as it happens. So let it be natural,' he told us.

I heard the telltale click of the camera recording and I moved toward Mollie, then hesitated and glanced down at my pants and the absence of any bulge. Not again. The fucker had better cooperate this time.

Noticing my scowl, Mollie followed my gaze. Without a word, she reached down and began rubbing me over the material of my slacks. 'Shh. No need to be nervous,' she said softly. 'Just relax. This is my job.' She leaned in to kiss me and I felt myself relax. And even better, I felt my dick stir to life. I kissed her back, adding some tongue until we were enthusiastically making out and the line between work and pleasure was definitely being crossed.

I moved her to the bed, unhooking her bra and tugging down her panties as we kissed.

And a few moments later, I was sinking inside her, all the standard foreplay I typically excelled at rendered unnecessary. Mollie rode me like the goddamn pro that she was, tossing her hair back and gripping my thighs as she lifted herself up and down on my cock.

I kept my eyes trained on her, needing to stay in the scene and not look at the crew who were glued to our performance. The strangeness of the whole situation ensured I wasn't going to blow too soon, something I'd been a little worried about.

My mind drifted unconsciously to Alexa and the way she looked in that little sundress. Her sweet innocence coupled with that feisty mouth of hers left me both turned on and confused. But I knew if I channeled my desire for Alexa into this performance, I would lose it. I opened my eyes and refocused on the girl in front of me.

Mollie moaned and gasped out high-pitched screeches that sounded incredibly fake. I was typically quiet during sex, preferring to hear the sounds of pleasure from the girl I was with, but her fake-sounding, over-the-top moans were grating on my nerves. Her screams built louder and I knew she was faking her orgasm. When her screams quieted to soft cries, her fake climax complete, all without any of the pleasure of feeling her pussy pulse around me, I pulled out and rolled her onto her stomach so I could fuck her from behind and finish this in relative peace.

Chapter 6

Alexa

Over the next several days, I couldn't get Cade out of my head no matter how hard I tried. It didn't help that I'd visited the porn website several times after finding he now had a video clip posted. I'd watched it numerous times, studying the way his hands explored the girl's body, and the rocking motion of his hips thrusting inside her, and the expressions of pleasure on his chiseled features. Each time I'd felt so dirty afterwards I'd had to scrub myself pink in the shower and bring some relief to my throbbing sexual need, all the while promising myself I wouldn't watch it again.

Remembering his gentle nature with his sister made me feel even worse about using him for my viewing pleasure. Yet I still couldn't keep my promise to myself about not watching the video. It was becoming a nightly routine, and had begun haunting my dreams. He still only had the one video clip, and I'd watched it so many times I now had it memorized. After realizing how silent Cade was, I watched it on mute from then on, not wanting to ruin it by listening to the girl's annoying screams.

In the days that followed, my thoughts drifted repeatedly to Cade's sweet little sister and the fierce determination that burned in her eyes. It broke my heart to realize they couldn't afford physical therapy, and I inadvertently found myself visiting the

41

physical therapy wing to ask a few questions of the therapist. It turned out that the severity of Lily's impairment could range from minor and not requiring much ongoing care, to severe, requiring lifelong physical therapy to help with flexibility and discomfort.

I didn't know which his sister had, but I had a pretty good notion that it was of the more serious nature, since she couldn't walk unassisted. I'd watched as the therapist worked with another child on one of those giant exercise balls and an idea planted itself firmly in my mind.

'Are you *insane*?' MacKenzie thrust the third paper cup of vending-machine coffee of the night at me. It was how we stayed awake and alert on the midnight shift.

I accepted the cup and dumped in a hefty dose of sugar, knowing the beverage needed it to make it drinkable. 'So says the woman who thought sleeping with him was a good idea. *That* would have been insane. I'm just talking about going to see him again. I can't stop thinking about that little girl, Kenz. And about how maybe I could help.'

She shook her head. 'Is this like the time you went to drop off groceries to the homeless people under the bridge and nearly got abducted, or the time you volunteered at the animal shelter and almost got eaten by that pit bull?'

'No,' I grumbled. 'This is nothing like that. I just want to drop by, check on them—I mean *her*—and see how I can help. He said he couldn't afford her physical therapy, Kenz. She deserves better.'

'News flash, you're not a physical therapist. You're a nursing student, Alexa.'

I tried a sip of the coffee, needing to get the caffeine in my system before my ten-minute break was over. Damn, still too hot. 'Close enough. I'll have to do. That is, if he'll even accept the help.'

'And this has nothing to do with seeing Cade again?' She cocked an eyebrow up at me suspiciously.

I focused on my coffee, stirring in another spoonful of sugar just for good measure.

'Because all that crap about sleeping with him? I was kidding, babe. You're sweet and beautiful. You deserve someone freakin' amazeballs. Not some animal who sells his body for money.'

'Amazeballs?' I questioned, looking up from my coffee.

'Ah-maze-balls,' she confirmed with a straight face.

I giggled at her. 'I've got to get back to work. Just trust me on this one, okay?' I downed a scalding gulp of the coffee and threw the cup in the trash on my way into the hall.

'It's your vagina!' she called after me, her voice carrying out into the hallway.

I cringed as the doctor passing by me perked up at the V word being shouted in our direction.

Maybe this was a stupid idea. After sleeping late, I'd showered and dressed casually in a pair of jeans and a simple black tank top, and then after making a stop at a sporting-goods store, I was currently parked in front of Cade's house once again.

I'd shown up the same time as before, thinking he'd be here to meet his sister off the bus again, but his pickup truck wasn't in the driveway.

I grabbed the exercise ball and pump from the backseat and made my way to house.

Moments later, an attractive girl answered the door. She looked to be around my age, maybe a year or two younger, and she was pretty with long blonde hair that hung down her back and wide-set gray eyes. My stomach dropped. Was this Cade's girlfriend?

Shit. Did porn stars have girlfriends? That would require a lot of trust. I mean, geez, he slept with other women for a living.

'Can I help you?'

I stood there for a second, still thrown off by this girl's appearance and the question of her relationship with Cade, until I realized I hadn't answered her yet. 'Is Cade home?'

She shook her head. 'He's working. Who are you?'

I swallowed down a lump in my throat. 'I'm Alexa, a…friend of his. And I brought this,' I held up the exercise ball, 'for Lily. I'm a nurse.' *Almost. Friend? Nurse? Geez, the lies were just spewing from my mouth.*

'Oh. Okay.' She opened the door wider. 'Lily will be home in a few minutes. You can come in and wait. I'm Becca, by the way.'

I followed her in the house, wondering what in the world I was doing and who the heck Becca was.

Chapter 7

Cade

I parked my truck and wondered where the hell Becca's car had gone. Had she taken Lily somewhere? I didn't like the idea of Becca driving Lily around in that deathtrap of hers. I grabbed my toolbox from the bed of the truck and stashed it in the garage before heading inside.

I was greeted by sounds of giggling coming from Lily's room. So Lily was here, but what about Becca? I stopped at the kitchen sink to wash the grime from my hands and then headed down the hall to find out what was going on.

The sight that greeted me wasn't at all what I was expecting. Lily was lying on a big exercise ball and Alexa was kneeling beside her, helping her to roll across the ball. I watched in stunned fascination for a second trying to understand what she was doing here and where the hell Becca had gone to.

'Caden!' Lily shrieked, spotting me in the doorway. She lifted herself from the ball on shaky legs, crossing the few steps without her walker and throwing herself into my arms.

'Hi baby doll.' I pulled her little body to mine in a brief hug. 'What are you guys doing?' I wanted to ask Alexa what the fuck she was doing in my house, but the grin on Lily's face calmed me.

45

'Lexa is teaching me some new exercises for my legs!' She returned to the ball, and bounced excitedly while Alexa grinned at her and held it steady. Lily's cheeks were flushed pink and I had to admit I hadn't ever seen her this excited to do her stretches. I just hoped she wasn't overdoing it.

'That's…nice. Um, Alexa, can I have a word with you in the other room?' I turned for the living room without waiting for her response.

'Stay here while I talk to Cade, okay?' I heard her say to Lily. She followed me into the living room, worry etched on her face.

'What are you doing here? Where's Becca?'

'I came over to see Lily and then Becca left.'

'She left? The person I'm paying to babysit her just left her, with… you. What are you even doing here?'

'It really isn't a big deal.'

'It's a big fucking deal to me.' I turned and faced the window, not wanting to lose my temper on her. Damn, I trusted Becca. How could she just leave Lily alone with a stranger?

'Hey.' Alexa's hand on my forearm caught my attention. 'I told her I was a friend of yours, and a nurse. I think she assumed…'

'That you were Lily's nurse?'

'Something like that.' She shrugged and removed her hand from my arm.

I blew out a breath and pressed the heels of my hands across my eyes. Fuck I was exhausted and dirty from working construction all day. I didn't expect to come home to this.

'I'm sorry, I wanted to help,' Alexa squeaked out in a soft voice. 'Becca left only five minutes before you got here. And she did try to call your cell, but she couldn't get through.'

I opened my eyes and met hers. Soft blue and wide with worry. Shit. I was being a dick. 'Listen, it's all right. Lily is safe and happy. I shouldn't have blown up at you like that. Finding good help to watch her is hard, and I don't think I'll be using Becca again, but that's not your fault.'

'Don't fire her on my account. It was just a misunderstanding,' she pleaded.

'I'll think about it. At the very least we'll be having a little talk about safety and strangers at the door.' I sighed, not wanting to argue with Alexa. 'Thanks for working with her today.'

She pulled in a breath and her shoulders visibly sagged with relief. 'You're welcome.'

'I can't afford a private nurse—'

'That's not why I came. You don't owe me anything.'

I cocked my head, studying her. 'Then why did you come?' I honestly hadn't expected to see her again, and now she was here, in my house, looking sexy in a pair of low-rise jeans and a fitted tank top that clung to her chest.

Alexa didn't get a chance to answer my question, because at that moment, Lily came barreling down the hallway, her walker clattering against the wood floor. 'I want Lexa!'

Alexa met my eyes and we both smiled. Lily's enthusiasm was contagious. 'Do you mind, um, staying with her for a few more minutes? I need to hop in the shower.' I looked down at my grimy jeans and T-shirt.

'Sure, not a problem.'

I kissed the top of Lily's head. 'Be good, okay?'

She nodded and lunged for me, wrapping herself around my leg in a hug. I winced, and bent over, moving her out of the way from clobbering my nuts. Alexa held in a laugh, realizing what I was doing. Then she headed back to her room with Alexa. I disappeared into the bathroom, completely confused at this turn of events.

Alexa was in my house, melting my damn heart by how sweet she was being with Lil.

I could hear happy sounds of conversation and laughter, and I poked my head out of the bathroom door to listen in.

'What does your brother like for dinner?' Alexa asked.

Lily took her time answering, and I held my breath, wondering what she'd say. 'Um, usually he likes to eat ice cream. And I do too.'

'You do, huh?' Alexa chuckled. 'Well let's find something healthy to make and maybe we can have ice cream *after* dinner.'

I took my time in the shower, my mind momentarily at ease that Lily was in good hands. I let the rough spray of water beat down on me, and closed my eyes.

After my shower, I threw on jeans and a T-shirt and made my way into a kitchen that was filled with amazing smells. Garlic. Tomatoes. Roasting meat. My mouth watered. It had been a long time since anyone had cooked for me.

Alexa was wiping down the kitchen counter, and I suddenly felt out of place in my own home. I didn't know whether to go in and help her, or see what Lily was up to.

Alexa spotted me, and made the decision. 'Dinner's ready. Get Lily for me?'

I nodded and found Lily in the living room, playing with the ball from earlier.

'Come on munchkin, let's eat.' I lifted her onto my hip, and carried her into the kitchen.

The table had been set with a big platter of spaghetti and meatballs, and a small cup of milk for Lily and a glass of ice water for me.

Lily stared in wonder at the place mats, napkins and dishes for two. Her stomach rumbled loudly and she slapped a little hand over her mouth and giggled.

Alexa's eyes caught mine and we both laughed.

'Hungry, little one?' I asked, settling her into her chair.

'Yep. And guess what?'

'What's that?' I placed a napkin over her lap.

'I helped Lexa roll the meatballs.'

'Oh yeah? I bet they'll be extra good then.'

She basked in the compliment. It was times like this, witnessing her sweet innocence and desire to belong, to fit in, that pulled at my heart and made every hour of hard work worth it.

Alexa gathered up her purse from the counter. 'I had fun with you today, Lily.'

'You're not staying?' I asked.

'Oh, no.' She looked down, adjusting the strap of her purse. 'You guys enjoy.'

'But you haven't had dinner yet, have you?'

She shook her head.

I stood and directed her towards the table. 'Sit.' I guided her into the chair next to mine then retrieved an extra plate and silverware from the kitchen, setting them in front of her. 'Here.' I scooped up a heap of spaghetti for Lily first, then some for Alexa.

'Oh, that's too much.' Alexa gestured to the full plate.

'Mine's too much too,' Lily said, grinning over at Alexa.

'Hush. Both of you girls are too thin. Eat up.'

I sat down and dug into my own plate, noting the satisfied smile tugging at Alexa's lips.

We enjoyed the delicious pasta and flavorful meatballs in relative silence. For once I didn't have to prod Lily to stop playing with her food and eat. She gulped the food down greedily and was soon coated from chin to cheeks in tomato sauce. I couldn't help but steal glances at Alexa throughout the meal, and I remembered that she hadn't answered my question earlier. I wondered just what, exactly, had prompted her to come over.

'We're going to need to hose you down out back, Lils,' I chuckled.

She slurped the noodle dangling between her lips and grinned. 'No way! I want Lexa to give me my bath tonight.'

A smile tugged at Alexa's mouth.

'Not tonight, baby doll. It's too late for a bath.'

Lily pouted but let it drop. Alexa exchanged looks with me across the table, and I could tell she wouldn't mind helping, but there was no way I was doing that to her. She'd already done too much.

Once we were through and Lily thoroughly wiped down, she escaped to play in her room while Alexa and I lingered at the table.

She tapped her fingers against the wood surface, studying me. 'So I take it you weren't shooting a new film today.'

'Ah, no. I work construction most days. That was just a… stupid mistake.'

'So you don't do it anymore?' she asked.

'I don't plan on it, but the money's damn good. And Lily's healthcare costs…' I shook my head. 'Never mind, I don't know why I'm telling you all this.'

She tucked her chin down, fiddling with her hands in her lap, not meeting my eyes.

'Are you through?' I nodded toward her plate.

'Yes, thank you.' She folded the napkin and set it on the empty dish.

I took our plates to the kitchen, and after a giving each a quick rinse, loaded them into the dishwasher. Alexa had cleaned as she cooked, because the dishwasher was loaded with the pots and implements she'd used while preparing supper. She leaned against the counter and watched me finish the rest.

'You said it was a mistake, but you did film one video…' Her voice trailed off and her eyes went wide, like she knew she'd been caught snooping.

My breath caught in my throat and my cock stirred in my jeans. 'You've seen it?' The idea of her watching me have sex with another woman was… incredibly fucking hot.

Her cheeks flushed crimson and I knew she'd not only seen it, but probably even gotten herself off while watching it. Ah, hell.

Chapter 8

Alexa

Lily's sudden appearance in the kitchen couldn't have come at a better time. I needed a heaping dose of *shut the hell up*. I'd practically admitted to Cade that I'd watched him on video. God, I probably sounded like a creeper. But that wasn't why I was here. It was this sweet little girl. The fact that her brother made me hotter than hell was beside the point.

I followed her to her room and helped her get undressed, removing her leggings and tunic while she kept one hand on her walker, holding herself up. I could tell that as she got tired, her coordination and muscle control went south. She pointed to the drawer where she kept her jammies, informing me that she wanted the Cinderella ones. I couldn't help but notice that the drawer also held a few gently worn, adult-sized T-shirts. Cade's I presumed. Those were probably full-length dresses on her.

I found the pink Cinderella nightgown trimmed in yellow lace and slipped it on over her head. I noted a small puckered scar from a recent surgery and a pronounced dimple where her spine had failed to fuse properly before birth. Poor little thing. I delicately touched the patch of skin, wishing my hands held the power to heal.

I lifted her into bed and secured the covers around her. 'Get some rest, sweet pea.' I brushed her blonde curls back from her

51

forehead and leaned in to press a kiss to the center of it. She smiled sleepily up at me, her eyes already beginning to fall closed.

'Night-night, Caden,' she whispered.

I turned and saw his large form filling the open doorway, his expression serious.

Cade remained silent, but his eyes were locked on me. Watching everything I did, my every movement with her. The intensity of his gaze sent a rush skittering along my spine. His look was both curious and possessive.

I crept from the room, and he backed away from the doorway, allowing me to close it behind us. I stood before him in the hallway, which suddenly felt crowded and narrow.

'You probably had better things to do than babysit all afternoon.' His voice was soft, careful.

'No, it's fine.' I couldn't believe I'd been here for going on six hours. The truth was it was nice being here, feeling helpful and needed. It was better than sitting alone in my empty apartment, studying.

He stepped in closer and lifted a hand to my cheek, brushing his thumb along the line of my jaw. 'Thanks for…taking care of her,' he said, his callused thumb whispering a delicate path along my skin.

I nodded, not trusting my voice to work.

'Do you have to go…or do you have time to stay for a drink?'

I nodded again.

'You have to go?' He dropped his hand.

'No, I can stay.'

A lazy grin tugged at the corner of his lips. 'Come on. I have beer, and I think I could even rustle up a bottle of wine.'

'Beer is fine.' Something icy to cool me off would be perfect.

I headed to the living room while he collected two bottles from the fridge and joined me on the couch. The beer was refreshing after such a long day, and I leaned back against the sofa, propping my feet up on the coffee table. He grinned at me, as if in agreement that it was tiring caring for her. I returned his smile, knowing she was worth every second of work.

I glanced around the sparse living room. No feminine touch here. No throw pillows, knick-knacks or candles, or any of the other things that made a house feel like a home. The room contained a large picture window efficiently covered with wooden blinds, a hunter-green sofa and armchair and a pair of matching coffee and end tables, one of which held a softly glowing lamp. It was sparse, but it was enough. You could tell this house was filled with love. It was completely at odds with how I first pictured Cade's life.

When I finally looked over at the man himself, I realized he was watching me from beneath hooded eyes. I took another sip of my beer and broke the connection. 'What is it?' he asked.

'You said you've had Lily since you were eighteen. I'm just wondering…what happened to your parents?'

He pulled back a healthy swig of his own beer before answering. 'That's too generous a term for them.'

I kept quiet, wrapping my fingers around the chilled bottle, waiting for him to continue.

'I was raised by my grandparents, and was left this house when they passed away. I was only seventeen, and my mother had given birth to a baby, and dropped the toddler off here. Lily wasn't walking yet and needed more care than they were prepared to give her.'

I couldn't help but compare how very different our lives were. My parents and I vacationed in Italy and spent Christmases at our ski lodge, and I never wanted for anything growing up—except for maybe more freedom. Cade was saddled with a special-needs child.

'I took one look at that little girl, and she stole my heart. I graduated from high school early and started working, determined to give Lily the life my parents couldn't. They were later busted for running a meth lab out of their trailer and are now in prison.'

Wow.

Sensing my inner turmoil, he gave my hand a squeeze. 'I promise you, we're managing.'

'I know, I can see that.' And they truly were. Cade, or Caden as Lily called him, was doing the best he could, providing a safe, loving home, even if he went about paying the bills in unconventional ways. Who was I to judge?

'Why'd you come today?'

I knew the question hadn't been forgotten. I hesitated for just a second before recovering. 'For Lily.' Which was mostly true.

He waited, eyeing me curiously. 'Are you sure that's all?'

Images from the sexy video replayed in my mind—the sensual curve of his mouth as he devoured hers with kisses. His large, rough hands softly caressing her skin. The skillful way his fingers spread her apart and rubbed slow circles in just the right spot. 'I... I don't know,' I breathed.

He rubbed a hand across the back of his neck, letting out a sigh. 'Fuck. Don't tempt me, Lex.' His voice was a rough plea in the silence of the room. The nickname on his lips felt far more intimate than it had any right to. Friends shortened my name all the time, but never before had it never made my heart jump.

I turned to face him on the couch, knowing this was crazy. He was a freakin' porn star. A bad boy with a capital B. Not someone I should crush on, but there it was all the same, pulsing in my chest. A want, a fierce desire I couldn't name. Something I definitely wasn't supposed to explore.

I wanted to be at the receiving end of that touch. I wanted to have those big hands, strong and calloused from working construction, yet still gentle, all over my body.

I wondered if it could be a simple infatuation, like the kind you developed for a movie star. I'd watched him in the most intimate of moments, so maybe my brain had created some type of freaky fascination that wasn't based on anything but his sexy body sending my sexless one into overdrive.

But when Cade turned to me and brought his hand up, cradling the back of my neck to pull me close to him and his waiting lips, all coherent thought escaped me.

He leaned in slowly, giving me time to pull away before his mouth captured mine in a scorching kiss. Oh, God, it was mouth-wateringly good. Slow and sensual, worshipping at my mouth, nipping at my lips, tasting me and making my sex wet and needy. My tongue darted out to lick his bottom lip and his responded in turn, colliding with mine in a tangle of wet heat. His fingers threaded themselves farther into my hair while his thumb traced slow circles on the sensitive skin at the back of my neck.

A mix of emotions flooded my system. Everything from desire over this sexy man to fear that Lily might catch us, to shame that to my parents would never approve of him as my boyfriend. I knew I was getting way ahead of myself even thinking like that when Cade stopped suddenly, and pulled back.

His eyes studied me, trying to understand what had just transpired between us. 'You're going to be the death of me, cupcake.' He brushed the dampness from my top lip with his forefinger.

I glanced down and caught sight of the huge bulge straining against his jeans. I pressed my lips into a tight line, trying to avoid grinning like a fool at the thought that I'd affected him just as much as he did me.

He lifted my chin with a single finger and made me meet his eyes. 'Hey, it's okay. Don't get shy on me now.'

I swallowed and relaxed into his hand. His thumb stroked my cheek and I automatically moved in to his caresses, my lids drowsily closing.

'That's better.' He smiled and dropped his hand. 'I don't know what's going on in that pretty head of yours, but if you ever really do want this, I'll be the one to do it. Hell, I'd be honored. But you should do it when you're ready, and with someone special.'

I nodded, sucking in my bottom lip so Cade wouldn't see it tremble.

'It's late. You should probably get going.' He stood and adjusted his erection. 'Come back and see Lily anytime.'

He ushered me to the door and out of the house, and if I didn't know better I would have thought he was trying desperately to get rid of me.

I drove home, exhausted, but most of all confused. But when I pushed the thoughts of Cade aside and remember Lily's little face smiling up at mine, or her determination to excel at each exercise I showed her, it tugged at my heart and I held onto those memories, wondering if I'd see either of them again.

Chapter 9

Cade

As badly as I wanted Alexa, she deserved better, especially for her first time. It wasn't right for her to just look for someone to get it over with. She wasn't that kind of girl. She deserved roses, candles, that kind of shit. And I was not that kind of guy.

I'd ushered her out of my house as quickly as I could without seeming like an asshole, my dick screaming in protest all the while. I wanted her like crazy. Just the thought of burying myself in her tight, wet heat was enough to drive me insane. Yes, I'd made the right decision sending her home. But dammit if I hadn't hid inside like some fucking pussy while she walked out to her car alone. I'd turned on the porch light and watched her from the window until she was safely inside her car and pulling away. I didn't trust myself to be near her just then.

It was for the best. At least that was what I told myself as I climbed into bed with a raging hard-on that refused to go away.

The following morning I met Ian at the gym once I got Lily off to school. All she talked about over breakfast was 'Lexa this and Lexa that.' Drove me up a fucking wall. I had a hard enough time keeping the woman out of my own thoughts, but with Lily now firmly planted on Team Alexa, it was near impossible.

I'd hoped lifting weights with Ian would clear my head, but so far it had proven difficult.

'What's got your panties in a twist?' Ian mocked me from a nearby weight bench. 'You're lifting like a pansy ass today.'

I sent him a *don't fuck with me* scowl and added another set of forty-fives to my bench press. I was struggling under the weight by the fourth rep. Damn.

Ian pulled the bar up and helped me re-rack it. 'Seriously, man. Talk to me.'

'This isn't Oprah, bro. Mind your own damn business.'

He chuckled and shook his head, leaving me alone on my bench. When I met up with him in the steam room, he kept true to the sentiment. He hadn't asked me any further questions about my shitty mood, and instead we talked strategy of his upcoming fight.

Ian was an up-and-coming mixed-martial-arts fighter. He was much better than me, and I was man enough to admit it. I also wasn't afraid to spar with him in the ring, even though he was lightning quick and his kicks ripped the air from your lungs. But my left hooks were nothing to fuck with, and I occasionally caught him off guard. More often than not, though, he didn't miss a blow—and my ribs had the bruises to prove it. Damn, he *had* to be good. He had a handful of local businesses sponsoring him, and had parents that had paid for every lesson imaginable growing up. He was born to do this. Me, on the other hand, I learned on the fly and won fights out of sheer determination.

Ian wiped the sweat from his eyes with a hand towel. 'So what about you? Are you planning on fighting again anytime soon?'

The money was pretty good—if you won. 'I don't know man, you try working construction with cracked ribs and a broken finger.' Not to mention trying to explain to a six-year-old why you were black-and-blue and watching her eyes well up with tears when you explained it was from a fight. It wasn't something I ever wanted to do again. She wanted to know who I fought with and why he was mad at me. I didn't like upsetting her like that. But it wasn't like I could say to my opponent, hey man, no face shots, my little sister gets upset. There was no way around the bumps and bruises—and even if I won, I'd still usually be sporting the distinctive look of a black eye for weeks.

One way or another, I needed to get my shit together and find a well-paying job that didn't require me to fight in a ring, or get naked on camera.

By the time I got home from the gym, Lily was due home from school. I had just enough time to make the phone call before I chickened out. I couldn't get Alexa and the way she'd left the night before off my mind. She'd done nothing but help out with Lily and I'd practically mauled her on my couch, told her I wanted to fuck her, and then sent her packing. I dialed the number to the hospital and asked to be connected to Alexa in nursing. I realized I didn't know her last name, but thankfully, a few minutes later, they tracked her down for me.

'Cade? Is everything okay…?'

Her voice was frantic. *Shit*. She'd probably assumed this call was about Lily. 'Everything's fine. Listen, I'll keep this quick because you're at work, but I needed to call and tell you I'm sorry if things got weird last night. That was my fault.'

She hesitated for a minute. 'That's okay. I had a lot of fun with Lily and—' she stopped short.

'Me too. Listen, can I return the favor? I'd like to make you dinner. Or at least buy you dinner, since you probably don't want me cooking.'

Soft feminine laughter filled the silence between us. 'Okay.'

'Are you free tomorrow night?'

'Yes. What time should I come over?'

I liked that she volunteered to come over, knowing it would be easiest for me and Lily if she came to my house again. Other girls I'd tried to date usually pitched a fit that I couldn't go out much. 'Six okay?'

'Yep. It's a date. I mean, I'll see you then.'

'Great. Oh, and I should probably get your number. You know, just in case I ever need help with Lily. You probably don't want me calling you at work. And I'll give you my cell number, in case you ever need anything too.' *Like me.*

'Okay,' she said softly. Just the sound of her voice brought out the alpha male in me. I knew being alone with her again probably wasn't a good idea, but I also knew I was powerless to stop it.

Chapter 10

MacKenzie and I sat in a corner booth in the hospital cafeteria, taking our lunch break. Well, we called it lunch, but it was three in the morning. I stuck with breakfast foods, while Kenz usually opted for dinner. The one thing we shared in common, though, was the consumption of mass quantities of coffee.

'Part of me does want to break out of my Little-Miss-Goody-Two-shoes image—do something crazy. Grasp onto experiences while I'm still young. I mean is that so bad?' I didn't mention Cade's invite to her to. I needed to test the water first.

'Amen, sister.' She raised her cup in a salute.

'I mean, would it be totally crazy if I wanted to, I don't know, mess around with Cade, see what all the fuss is about…'

MacKenzie spit out a mouthful of coffee. 'I didn't realize we were talking about that!' I mopped the warm liquid from the table in front of her with a stack of napkins. 'You do what you want, babe. But you do know he's not going to be satisfied with straight vanilla sex, right? He's probably done things we've only dreamed about.'

I didn't know what her dreams consisted of, but vanilla sex was the extent of mine. 'Like?'

'Threesomes, orgies, anal sex…'

61

I held up my hand, stopping her. 'Okay. Enough, thanks.' My cheeks flamed at her tirade. I was interested in exploring my sexuality with Cade, but there was no way I was ready for any of that. I couldn't even hear the words without blushing.

MacKenzie chuckled. 'Relax, Lex. I told you. He'd be freakin' lucky to get a girl like you. I still think you're too good for the likes of him, but that's my opinion. Just promise me one thing if you really are set on this.'

Was I set on this? I wasn't sure. The only thing I was sure about—Cade provoked strange reactions in my body. 'What's that?'

'Have your fun with the porn star, but promise me that you won't involve your heart.'

I nearly laughed at her ridiculous warning. My heart? I wanted to assure MacKenzie that there was no possibility of me falling for Cade, but my mind flickered back to his gentle nature with Lily and the words stuck in my throat. I nodded my consent. 'My parents set me up with another son-in-law candidate. His name's Peter and he's taking me to lunch tomorrow.'

She rolled her eyes. MacKenzie was well-briefed in my parents' meddling ways. 'Okay. Can I give you one tip, in all seriousness, if you're going to do this?'

'Sure.'

'You'll want to shave everything—thoroughly—he's used to those girls in the videos, and you won't find a speck of hair anywhere on them.'

I rolled my eyes. This was her advice? I wasn't about to shave off all my pubic hair just to appease a man. Was I?

'I've got to get back to work.' I tossed the cup into the trash and stuffed the last bite of bagel into my mouth.

Why I'd agreed to a date with Peter Wyndham III today was beyond me. It was a moment of weakness—my mom had caught me coming off the high of spending time with Cade, and I'd agreed.

I'd first met Peter at last year's Christmas party at my dad's office. The same party where they'd paraded me around like a prized possession since the day I turned eighteen. As if I wanted a fat, bloated accountant for a husband. Thankfully Peter had been different. He was twenty-four, fresh out of business school, and felt just as out of place with the middle-aged accountants and their spouses as I did.

We'd spent the evening sitting on a balcony, me with his suit coat draped across my bare shoulders talking about our favorite college courses—mine, philosophy, and his, economics.

My parents had been delighted to see us hit it off. He was a prized catch in their eyes, everything they wanted for me—a white male aged twenty to thirty, good genetics, well-bred, from an upper-middle-class New Hampshire family. Wholesome as a glass of milk. And just as exciting.

Their excitement alone caused me to squirm. I'd avoided his calls and their feeble attempts to set us up for the better part of six months. Which was why I found it baffling that I was currently curling my hair, and ironing my navy shirtdress, getting ready for my date.

We'd made plans to play tennis at the country club where both he and my father were members. I packed my tennis outfit into my large purse, which MacKenzie had named the Mary Poppins bag and went to wait for Peter.

When he pulled up in his sleek silver Lexus, I jogged out to meet him. Peter emerged from the car, all gelled blonde hair and straight white teeth indicating years of orthodontia. He met me at the car door, dressed casually in jeans and a button-up shirt and kissed the back of my hand before helping me inside the car. The rich smell of leather enveloped me and I settled back in my seat.

Something about Peter was familiar, like a pair of worn-in jeans, or your comfy flip flops, but nothing about his presence—and certainly not his kiss—brought me anywhere close to fireworks. More like tolerable indifference. Cade on the other hand…well, my nipples pebbled at the mere thought of him.

After an uninspired tennis match, which he'd predictably let me win, we had lunch on the spacious stone patio at the club. I ordered a champagne strawberry salad and Peter the truffle risotto. We sipped sparkling water while we ate and Peter told elaborate stories designed to impress me. He began with adventures on his father's sailboat, crazy parties with his friends from prep school, and finally his career ambitions—to make partner by the age of thirty-five. Never once did he ask about mine. Or anything about me, really. I found my mind wandering to Cade and Lily. I wondered what they did on the weekends. I imagined chocolate-chip-pancake breakfasts eaten in pajamas while watching cartoons. The thought made me smile. I couldn't help the occasional glances down at my watch, counting down the minutes until this date was over and I could go see Cade and Lily.

After our date, Peter walked me out to my car, opening the door while I settled in to the driver's seat.

'That was fun. We should do it again. My family does this wine tour every fall, you should come.'

'I'll think about it,' I said, then pulled my car door closed.

Chapter 11

Cade

I got home from work just moments before six. Ian's younger sister, Sophia, who was nineteen and taking classes at the nearby community college often babysat for me and had been here since three to see Lily off the bus.

I wandered inside and found Lily eating dinner at the table, and Sophia sitting with her, filing her nails.

'Caden!' Lily dropped her fork and was in my arms in seconds.

'Did you do your exercises?' I kissed the top of her head.

'Not yet. Me and Sophia were playin'.'

I frowned at Sophia. She shrugged and mumbled an apology, rising up to greet me with a hug. 'Mmm, someone smells good.' She buried her nose in my neck.

'Don't. I have a…date coming over.' After work, I'd gotten in a quick workout with Ian and showered at the gym before coming home.

'You? A date?' Sophia narrowed her eyes in disbelief. 'You don't date. Lord knows I've been trying to get you to ask me out for years.'

'Sophia…' I gently steered her away by her shoulders, adding some distance between us. 'You know Ian would have my balls if I laid so much as a finger on you.' Which was entirely true, but it was more than that. Sophia had grown in to a beautiful young woman, the problem was, when I looked at her, I still saw the gangly ten-year-old girl whose Barbie dolls regularly became Ian's and my prisoners of war.

'We could work around that and you know it. Ian isn't the boss of me.' Sophia smiled, batting her eyelashes, resting her hand on my forearm. Oh, I definitely knew sure she'd be more than happy to work around it.

She'd been trying for months to get me to notice her, cleaning my house in her tiny cut-off shorts, and offering to watch Lily for me at any time of the day or night. And even though I knew her motives, I let her do it. If that made me a dick, then so be it. I wasn't about to refuse her help. We both knew I needed it, though I'm sure she held on to hope I'd change my mind about her. About us.

'Finish your dinner, Lily. I have company coming over tonight.'

'Is Lexa comin' back?' Lily's face broke out into a grin when I nodded.

'Who's Lexa?'

Who was Alexa? That was a very good question. A girl I had no shot in hell with in real life. A girl who had the face of an angel and the body to rival any porn star. Someone sweet to my sister and probably capable of destroying my heart in the process. 'Just a friend,' I said.

Sophia rolled her eyes. 'Uh huh, friend my ass.' She slapped a palm over her mouth. 'I meant bottom.' She looked down at Lily who was now giggling. 'I'll clean up for you a little. Go get ready for your date, stud.' She slapped me on the ass.

'Thanks, Soph.' I shuffled off to the laundry room, dropping my damp gym clothes into the washer. 'Did you pick up your room, Lils?' I called from down the hall. I tried as much as possible to treat her like a regular kid. I wanted her to grow up independent and self-reliant, not thinking she was any different than anyone else, or incapable of taking care of herself. After all, the day would come when I wouldn't be there to help her. And that was something I didn't even want to think about.

I heard her scamper off to her room and I smiled to myself as I started the washer.

When I walked into the living room Sophia had thrown her hair up in a ponytail and had shed her baggy sweatshirt, leaving her in a skin-tight T-shirt and pair of jeans. She was flitting around the house, dusting the living room, picking up stray items and generally making the house presentable.

I had a feeling she was only sticking around to size up the girl I supposedly had a date with. I wasn't even sure this was a date. I didn't know what had prompted me to say that. Maybe because I knew Alexa wasn't the kind of girl you screwed around with casually.

A knock at the front door sent a prickle down the back of my neck, raising the hair there and lighting all my senses in anticipation.

Sophia jogged to the door, but I stopped her from opening it. 'Let me.'

She stepped back and placed her hands on her hips. 'Of course.'

I shook my head and took a deep breath, then pulled open the door. Alexa looked stunning. She wore a short-sleeved navy-blue dress that hugged her curves, and fell just above her knees. Her legs were tanned and tone, and ended in sexy feet encased in a pair of silver sandals. She looked sexy and innocent all at once. 'Come in.' I stepped back to allow her inside. Sophia cleared her throat from behind me, and I dragged my gaze from Alexa.

'This is Sophia—a friend of mine and Lily's,' I gestured to the young woman. It didn't escape my notice that she and Alexa were having a strange staring contest, sizing each other up. 'Sophia was just leaving. Thanks for today, Soph.'

A smile crept across her lips, a smug look on her face. 'Same time tomorrow?'

'No, I've got it covered. Besides, I don't like you missing class to take care of Lily for me.'

She grabbed her purse and sweatshirt from the couch and secured her bag across her body. 'Caden James, you know I'd do just about anything for you.' She smiled at me wickedly. It wasn't lost on me that she was trying to imply, for Alexa's sake, there was more to our friendship. There wasn't. Never had been, never would be, despite how much she tried to tempt me.

Once Sophia was gone, Alexa fidgeted nervously in the entryway, playing with the strap of her purse. I took her by the shoulders. 'Hey, she's my best friend's little sister. That's all. Okay?'

She nodded obediently, her voice barely a whisper, 'Okay.' She stepped out of her strappy heels, leaving her several inches shorter and followed me inside.

Lily came clattering down the hall just then and Alexa dropped to her knees to encase her in a giant hug. Lily chattered on about her day and Alexa nodded and giggled, pausing to ask questions. It was startling to see how much Lily looked up to Alexa already. It was sweet and at the same time concerning. If Alexa didn't stick around, I knew I'd have one heartbroken little girl on my hands.

I asked Alexa if she was okay if we got Lily settled in for the night, and she nodded and then went to help Lily with her stretches. Alexa sat on the floor with Lily, showing her a couple of new ways to stretch her back and legs. The build-up of watching Alexa was like a slow torture, the lingering glances, the casual brushes against her skin, and finally we were tucking Lily into bed.

Alexa followed me down the hallway toward the living room. I watched her take a tentative step toward where I was seated on the couch. All the oxygen was sucked from the room, the air thick with tension, now that our pint-sized chaperone was soundly asleep.

Having her here with me—with Lily—was fucking with my head. I couldn't even begin to understand her motives.

Alexa fidgeted in the doorway, as if pausing for my inspection. Her dress ended just above her knees, and my gaze traveled up and down her bare legs.

'You look nice.' My voice was gruff.

'I had a date.'

She'd been on a date today and the asshole had let her leave? Dressed like that? Her bare legs were toned and tan, her toenails painted pale pink. She was stunning.

'Come here,' I instructed.

She obeyed, crossing the room to stand in front of me, her wide eyes cast down to meet mine. I trailed a single fingertip over the back of her bare leg, and felt her shudder under my touch.

'So tell me about this date you had.' I continued lazily stroking the soft flesh behind her knee.

She swallowed and drew a deep breath. 'He took me to his country club for tennis and then lunch on the terrace.'

'And now you're here slumming it with me?' I felt her knees lock to keep herself steady. 'I don't do roses and candles and country clubs. Dates with me wouldn't involve tennis.' I wasn't sure quite why I was pushing her, only that I wanted her honesty, so I supplied her with the same treatment.

'No?' she challenged, finding her voice, however faint.

'No, cupcake. I'm more of a beer and hot wings, and sex in the cab of my truck kind of guy.' She sucked in a quick intake of breath and her knees trembled. I wrapped both hands around the backs of her legs to keep her from collapsing. 'But for you I could probably make an exception.' Her gaze held mine and the air grew thicker around us.

'But what if I like that beer and hot wings idea?' she challenged.

I noted that she conveniently left out the part about sex, and I knew I shouldn't, but damn, I wanted to see her reaction. 'I meant the exception would be that instead of my truck, I'd want you spread out in my bed where I could fuck you properly.'

She let out a soft whimper and her legs gave out completely. I hauled her onto my lap, rather than letting her collapse in a heap on the floor.

'I've got you,' I breathed against her hair. Her heart was fucking pounding, and I could see her pulse thrumming against her neck. It was a major turn on. I tilted her chin, pulling her in until her lips met mine and I softly kissed her. 'Tell me what you want, Alexa.'

'I can't.'

I frowned. 'Can't or won't?' She swallowed and looked down. We were going to have to work on that. Bur first things first. 'Let's eat something.' I moved her from my lap so she was seated next to me on the couch. 'Shall we stay in or I could try and find a babysitter to come over...'

'Let's stay in.'

'I usually order out after I put Lily to bed. What would you like?'

'Whatever you usually have is fine.'

'Well there's always beers and chicken wings...' I grinned and raised an eyebrow. This was *so* not a beer and wings kind of girl.

But without missing a beat, she smiled and nodded. 'Sounds good to me.'

'Are you okay with some heat?'

She nodded, ignoring the innuendo. 'Just as long as it's not too spicy.'

'I think you can handle it.' I met her eyes and held them. Her big blue eyes widened and met mine. The sweet way she didn't back down and her sincere curiosity about this thing between us stirred something inside me.

I pulled out my phone to order. 'Hey, Billy. Yeah, actually make it two orders of my usual.' I stood up and crossed the room. 'You okay to wait here while I go pick up the food? It'll only take a few minutes.'

'Sure.'

When I returned with a six-pack of beer and the cartons of food, Alexa had gathered napkins and plates from the kitchen. We settled on the couch again to eat.

I opened the containers of wings and celery sticks, placing them on the coffee table. 'Have as much as you want.'

'Thanks.' She eyed the food suspiciously before daintily placing a napkin across her lap. 'I've never actually eaten a chicken wing before,' she admitted.

'Ever?'

She shook her head.

Damn. This girl really was in a totally different league. She probably never ate anything that didn't require utensils. I wanted to tell her she didn't have to worry about getting messy in front of me, but she surprised me by digging right in, lifting a chicken wing from the container and curiously looking it over as if wondering how to begin.

I watched as she carefully as she nibbled at the meat, getting sauce on her bottom lip and fingertips in the process. 'Mm. It's good.' She sounded surprised. Watching her lick the sauce from her fingers was doing wicked things to my groin.

'Good.' I shoved the napkins towards her. 'Now eat.'

She kept stealing glances at me from the corner of her eye, but we ate in relative silence. I removed a beer from the six pack and offered it to her. 'Would you like one?'

She nodded. I twisted off the top and handed her the open bottle. She immediately brought it to her lips, likely to wash away the heat from the food. The wings were spicier than usual, but she didn't complain.

'You mind if I turn on the game?' I asked, reaching for the remote.

She was digging into another wing and gave a half nod.

I flipped on the game, more for the background noise than anything else.

Alexa leaned forward in her seat. 'What's the score?'

'You like football?' I couldn't help the surprise straining my voice.

She nodded. 'I love the Bears. Watching football was the one normal thing I did with my dad.' She smiled.

Oh. A girl that likes hot wings and beer, and now she tells me she a Bears fan too. *Lord have mercy.* My resolve to stay away from her just got more interesting.

We finished eating and I cleared away the food, but Alexa instructed me to leave the beer. We were each on our second, and the fact that she was a lightweight was evident by the way she leaned back against the couch, tucking herself against my side.

She was more entertaining than the game, freely yelling at the TV whenever the ref made a bad call. I watched the way she tilted the bottle to her lips and took a long pull, her graceful neck moving as she swallowed. She slipped her feet up on the couch bedside us, and I pulled them over to my lap. The contact caught her attention and she shifted so she was facing me.

'Cade?' she whispered in the dimly lit living room.

'You've eaten. Now it's time we had our talk, cupcake.' I started gently rubbing her feet. 'Tell me what you want.'

She leaned over and set her beer bottle on the coffee table before returning to face me. She bit her lip as if unsure of herself, and looked everywhere but at me.

'This. You. I want you to…teach me.' She swallowed, her tongue darting out to taste her bottom lip.

Did she know what she was asking of me? Could she possibly understand? 'Teach you what?'

'How to…please you…'

I lightly grasped her chin with my fingertips and lifted her face so I could meet her eyes. 'How to make me come?'

'Y-yes,' she whimpered.

She leaned forward and planted a sweet kiss on my mouth and my dick leapt to life in my jeans. She wanted to understand how to please a man, but her sexy innocence guaranteed she wasn't going to have to try too hard. I needed to get myself in check before I hauled off her panties and showed her exactly what to do.

Chapter 12

Alexa

Cade lifted me onto his lap, arranging me so I was straddling him, my dress hitched up around my legs. He trailed his fingertips along my exposed thigh, tracing a lazy pattern. 'You sure you want this?' he whispered.

My heart was pounding so hard I thought it was about to burst through my ribcage. I could feel his erection pressing into the apex of my thighs. I did want this, didn't I? Wasn't this why I was here? God, I was confused.

'You hesitated,' he breathed against my neck before pulling back to meet my eyes.

'I know.'

He straightened my dress around me, ensuring I was still covered. 'Listen, we don't have to do anything you're not comfortable with.' He continued to tease me, tracing a finger farther up my thigh, inching deliciously closer to the edge of my panties.

I whimpered.

'I want you. You have no idea how fucking badly. But you'll set the pace, okay?'

I nodded. 'Okay.' I instantly felt better, relieved and sure of what I wanted and didn't want. 'No sex…but can we do some um, other stuff?'

He chuckled, a deep throaty laugh rumbling through his chest. 'Anything you want, baby.'

Crap. I probably sounded so awkward. I didn't know the right way to approach this. But luckily, Cade took the lead and didn't make me vocalize what I wanted.

His mouth captured mine in a deep kiss, and my tongue was soon following his lead, caressing and tangling with his.

I tried not to compare Cade's every movement to those of his video, but it was difficult. The images replayed in my head, but so far, this moment was uniquely ours. His fingers skittered along my calves and up over my knees, spreading them apart just slightly so he could press even closer to me.

'What about Lily?' I asked between kisses.

'She's asleep.'

'What if she wakes up?'

'We'll hear her.' He continued kissing me.

I supposed he was right. We'd hear her walker moving across the wood floor.

He unbuttoned my dress slowly, taking his time to kiss and nip at my lips, neck and collarbone with each button he successfully freed. By the time he was lifting the dress over my head, I raised my arms dutifully, allowing him to pull it off. I thrust my ample chest out for his inspection.

His eyes flooded with desire as he looked me over. 'Goddamn, cupcake.' I looked down at my white bra, wishing I'd listened to MacKenzie's advice about buying new lingerie, but Cade didn't seem the least be hampered by my white cotton bra and panties. I was glad I'd taken her advice and shaved today.

Cade's thumbs grazed across my nipples. I let out a throaty groan. He continued his torturous strokes along my breasts, his fingers dipping into the cleavage and sliding across the hardened tips. I wondered if he was going to remove my bra, or if maybe he was waiting for me to do that.

75

'You said you wanted to know how to please me?' He tilted my chin up to meet his eyes. 'Consider this lesson number one. Don't be afraid to ask for what you want. Hearing you say it is a major turn on.'

I sucked in a breath and held it. No way I'd be good at dirty talk. It'd be like asking me to speak a different language. I couldn't even vocalize what I wanted in plain English.

His hands dropped from my chin and gripped both breasts, roughly palming them. 'I've been dreaming about your tits for weeks now. Seeing them bouncing above me as you rode my cock.'

I let out a moan at his words, a flood of heat dampening my sex.

Cade smirked as if in victory. 'You try.'

My nerves were back as I tried to think. I squirmed in his lap and felt the firm ridge pressing against me. Before I even realized it, I was blurting out, 'I love the feel of your hard dick.' God I sounded stupid. But Cade's head dropped back against the sofa and he closed his eyes, as if savoring my words. I instantly felt proud.

He guided me to his mouth by the back of my neck, threading his fingers in my hair. 'You want to play with it?'

I nodded, unable to form words.

He smiled against my lips. 'Good girl. But not yet. First I need to make you come.'

Need? *To make me come?* Oh…

He reached around for the back clasp of my bra and released it with a single flick, then eased the straps down my shoulders and discarded it on the floor beside us.

His mouth joined his hands in the loving caresses, licking and suckling my hardened peaks. I grabbed his hair and thrust my chest toward his eager mouth, wanting more. 'Oh God that feels good,' I moaned.

Before I had time to examine what was happening, he flipped me over so that I was lying on my back on the couch and he was kneeling on the floor beside me pulling my panties down my legs.

'I want to hear you screaming my name…' he whispered against my inner thigh.

That was so not happening. I was hyper aware of not wanting to wake up Lily. Geez. At least one of us was thinking clearly.

He dipped his fingers between my thighs, lightly running his fingertips up the length of my folds. 'You're soaking wet, baby.' His voice was rough, barely in control.

I bit my lip and opened my thighs wider, allowing him to explore, long past feeling self-conscious.

He eased one long finger inside me, and slid it in and out with gentle pressure. 'Do you like that, cupcake?' He laid a gentle kiss just below my navel.

I whimpered in response.

His eyes stayed locked on mine and he added a second finger. 'So tight, so beautiful,' he murmured.

'More, please,' I pleaded.

He groaned and pumped his fingers harder, driving into me until I was panting and writhing under his talented hand. Then he eased himself down, sweeping his tongue over my sex and my world shattered. The wet heat from his mouth exploded around me, the sensation causing my hips to buck off the couch. 'Cade!' I gasped. *Crap*. So much for not screaming. I didn't care. I lifted my hips to meet his mouth and rode out the pulsing wave as an intense orgasm erupted through my core. I opened my eyes and found Cade's eyes still locked on me.

'You're beautiful,' he whispered.

I swallowed and lifted myself up into a sitting position, suddenly feeling insecure about my nakedness. Cade was still fully dressed.

His hand on my arm stopped me. 'Where do you think you're going?'

I looked down at his crotch and was alarmed to see the large bulge clamoring to be released. I licked my dry lips. 'Can I just have my panties?'

His lips curved in the tiniest of smiles, but he lifted them gingerly from the floor. 'If it'll make you more comfortable. But your top stays off.' He read the back of the underpants. 'Sunday, huh?'

I snatched them from his grasp and slipped them up my trembling legs. 'Are you going to show me...what to do...?' I looked down at his groin.

He chuckled and sat down next to me on the couch, lacing his fingers behind his head. 'Knock yourself out, sweetheart.'

I unbuckled his belt with fumbling fingers then released the button and zipper. A smile pulled at my mouth at the small victory and Cade leaned forward to kiss me.

He lifted his hips as I tugged down his jeans and boxers. His thick, rigid cock sprang free to greet me and I sucked in a deep breath. 'You're still shaved,' I murmured. I wondered if he was going to be starring in another video any time soon. The thought both excited and bothered me.

A smile crossed his lips. 'Tell me something...you watched my video, right?'

I looked down.

'Answer me.' He tilted my jaw up, running his fingers along the length of my throat.

I nodded.

'How many times?' His voice was low and rough.

I shrugged. Even if I could have found my voice, I didn't know the answer to that question. It was too many to count.

'Did you touch yourself?'

I nodded again.

'Fuck, that's hot.' His rough voice sent a flood of moisture to my panties. 'Show me,' he commanded.

Summoning my courage, I slipped off my panties and brought my hand down between my legs, gripping his thigh with my other hand since I was still balanced on my knees. Cade kept his eyes locked on mine before slowly lowering them to where my hand was rubbing gentle circles over my clitoris. He sucked in a breath and held it.

'Damn baby, that's about the prettiest thing I've ever seen.'

I smiled crookedly up at him and dropped my hand, suddenly feeling unsure. Some things were just meant to be done in private. 'It feels better when you do it,' I admitted.

He leaned forward and kissed me, easing his hand in between my legs. 'Yeah?' His middle finger slid easily inside me.

'Yeah...' I groaned at the sudden fullness.

He flicked his finger along my inner wall and I almost crumbled to the floor. I gripped his legs to remain upright. 'My fingers are longer,' he whispered. 'I can reach your G-spot.' He nipped my lips in a quick kiss, massaging the spot again and again. My nails dug into his legs. 'Just wait until I'm inside you,' he whispered.

I whimpered.

'Not tonight, cupcake.'

I moaned in protest. 'Cade.'

'Shh.' His finger continued its torturous ministrations. 'I'm not fucking you tonight.'

I winced at his use of the term. 'You mean make love?'

His finger stilled inside me. 'No, I mean fuck. If you want to make love, you go see your country-club boy, if you want to be properly fucked, you come to me.' His voice was rough. 'But not until you're ready. Not until you ask me.'

I nodded, knowing he was right. I wasn't ready, but that didn't mean I wanted him to stop, especially when I was so close again.

Cade slowly began working his long digit against that sensitive spot once again. I gripped his thighs and I squeezed my eyes closed as an intense pressure built inside me and eventually blossomed into an earth-shattering orgasm. He let out a low tortured groan watching me with desire burning in his eyes. My eyes fell closed in complete bliss as I rode out the sensations.

Suddenly I couldn't wait any longer to touch him. I leaned forward and trailed a path of soft, damp kisses along his shaft. His scent was musky and decidedly male, and I wanted more. I craved it in a way that was primal and entirely new to me.

I eased the head into my mouth, and suckled at the smooth skin. His breath released in a hiss from between his teeth. My hands joined in the fun, stroking up and down as I devoured the length of him.

'Damn, baby.' He groaned, his head dropping back against the couch.

I never knew this could be so pleasurable, but I found myself getting lost in the rhythm, sucking and licking and trailing my hands along his shaft.

'Just like that, angel. Stroke it.' He watched my hands work up and down his length and groaned a deep growl low in his throat. My heart jumped. Hearing those sounds come out of him was so sexy. 'I'm going to come,' he gasped.

Seconds later, hot jets of semen exploded down the back of my throat and Cade released a final groan.

A satisfied smile crossed his lips and he looked down at me with wonder. 'Damn baby, you didn't have to swallow it.' He stroked my jaw with his thumb, studying me carefully.

It wasn't like I'd had a well-thought-out plan. I'd just done what I needed to do. I wasn't about to go running for the bathroom, my behind jiggling in his face as I jogged away. No thank you. Besides, it hadn't been that bad.

He smiled a sleepy grin. 'In case you're wondering…that felt fucking amazing.'

I no longer blanched at his overeager use of the F-bomb, it only endeared him to me more. Cade was all male. There'd be no changing him, no tempering his ways. Maybe it was my strict upbringing, but something inside me envied that.

Warmth flooded my cheeks at his compliment, and I lifted my chin to meet his eyes. He continued tracing lazy circles along my cheek, working his hand behind my hair to massage my neck, not bothering to tuck his softening cock back inside his pants. Since he didn't care about our semi-nude state, I relaxed into his caresses, resting my head on his thigh.

'That feel good, cupcake?' he whispered.

'Mm-hm,' I mumbled, tilting my head to give him better access. His fingers reached nearly all the way around my neck and he used a strong but soothing pressure. I would go down on him every day if it meant getting a massage like this afterwards. I relaxed into his touch and soaked up the loving attention.

Several minutes later, and on the verge of falling asleep, I stood and redressed. Cade straightened his clothes, pressed a quick kiss to my lips and then went down the hall, I assumed to check on Lily. Above all else, he was a good big brother, and that was all that really mattered.

Unsure of what to do with myself, I gathered up the empty beer bottles and brought them to the kitchen to rinse them out. I set them on the counter by the sink, wondering where he kept the recycling bin, or if he had one at all. Cade entered the kitchen behind me.

'Just leave it. I'll clean up in the morning.' He pressed a kiss to the back of my neck and I turned to hug him, comforted by his warm embrace. 'Let me walk you out. I want to make sure you get to your car safe and sound.'

I didn't comment that my car was only thirty feet away, I simply nodded and allowed him place his hand on my lower back and escort me to the door. Maybe it had something to do with us sharing chicken wings, and football, and oral sex. Whatever it was that had brought out his protective streak, I wasn't about to complain. It was nice.

Chapter 13

Cade

Having Alexa's willing body that close nearly sent me over the edge. Watching her small hand close around my shaft had sent a throbbing rush of blood to my cock. Was I crazy enough to believe that something would become of this, other than a friendship centered around Lily and the side benefits of worshipping her sweet body once the sun went down? Surely she had to realize that I didn't fit into her life, not by a long shot. But I'd take what I could get, for as long as I could have it.

That night I fell asleep to the memory of Alexa's gentle voice reading from Lily's favorite book, and the way she animated the voices of each different character to make Lily chuckle. With a sleepy smile planted on my lips, I rolled over and fell asleep.

On Saturday Alexa called and asked if she could pick up Lily for a girls day. After I recovered from my stunned silence, I'd agreed. This girl continued to level me. It was like she knew the way to my hardened heart—through Lily. Maybe I never considered a serious relationship before because no one had ever shown an interest in developing a relationship with Lily too. Once they found out about my sister, they usually bailed.

An hour later, Lily chanted Lexa's name as she watched the little BMW SUV pull up alongside the curb. We met Alexa on the sidewalk. 'So what are you girls up to today?'

'Well, I was thinking I'd leave it up to Miss Lily. We could have a beauty day at the spa, or we could go to this boutique where you get to choose a ceramic figurine to paint.'

'Yeah!' Lily's face lit up.

'Which one, baby doll? You have to choose.' Alexa's generosity was too much as it was.

Lily's face scrunched up in concentration for a moment before she looked up at Alexa. 'Can we do both?'

Alexa grinned that crooked smile I'd grown fond of and nodded. 'Sure can, sweet pea.'

I helped buckle Lily in the backseat and placed her walker in the rear cargo space, then meet Alexa at the driver's door. 'You sure you're okay with this?'

'Absolutely. Go enjoy your Saturday. Just keep the booty calls to a minimum.' She patted my chest.

'Will do.'

I watched them drive away. The little girl who owned my heart and the beautiful Alexa who was pulling it in an entirely new direction.

I took advantage of the rare opportunity for an extra gym session with Ian, but coming home to an empty house felt too weird. After about an hour of aimless pacing and puttering I decided to call Alexa and check on them. Maybe she was going crazy. It was definitely time to check on her. I dialed her cell and she answered on the first ring.

'Hi Cade.' She sounded out of breath. 'We finished at the ceramics place and grabbed some lunch. What's up?'

I heard a squeal of laughter in the background. 'Where are you guys?'

'At the spa just down the road. Is it okay if Lily gets her hair cut? It'll just be a trim.'

'Ah, sure.' My neighbor lady usually cut it, but what the hell. 'Where are you guys? I could swing by and see Lily.'

'Sure. She'd love that I'm sure.' She gave me the directions and I set off in my truck, needing to get out of my too-quiet house.

When I walked in the spa, I was greeted by the sounds of new age music mixed in with bird calls and the babble of water, and the scent of lavender that was so strong it slapped me in the face.

I turned a corner and found Alexa and Lily seated in a large chairs, their feet propped up in front of them.

'Caden!' Lily squealed once she spotted me.

They wiggled their pink toenails at me. I wasn't sure what I was supposed to be noticing. 'Look at that. Two very pretty girls.'

They smiled at my compliment, so it appeared I'd said the right thing and we made our way to the front.

'Here.' Alexa handed me her credit card. 'Will you check us out? I want to run over to the bakery next door. I'll just be a minute.'

'Sure.' I took the card, but planned to pay with my own once Alexa was outside. She'd done too much for us already. But when the girl at the counter told me the bill came to three-hundred dollars, I reluctantly handed over Alexa's card. Three hundred dollars for toenail polish and a couple of haircuts? Their hair didn't even look any different to me. One thing was clear—Alexa led a lifestyle I'd never be able to afford. And I sure as shit didn't need Lily getting used to this kind of treatment.

Alexa came back a few minutes later carrying a little pink pastry box, looking smug. She signed the credit card slip and took her card from the counter, then headed outside to her car with Lily in tow. 'See ya back at the house,' she called.

I stood by uselessly until they drove away, then stomped off to my truck. I stopped on the drive home to pick up dinner for the three of us, needing to do something to get things back under control.

Once I got home I could hear Lily singing and playing in her bedroom and found Alexa sitting on the couch waiting for me. I set the bags of food on the table and turned to her. 'You didn't have to do all that today.' My voice came out sterner than I intended.

She stood and placed her hands on her hips. 'I know that, Cade. I wanted to. I never had a little sister. Did you ever think that maybe I like spending time with her?'

Shit. I sounded like a real prick. I rubbed the back of my neck. 'Sorry, it's just this is new for me.' There was no denying that the way Alexa was with Lily complicated things between us. It twisted my insides, and brought out my protective instincts.

Her expression softened. 'It's new for me too.' She leaned her hip against the counter, drawing herself unconsciously closer to me.

I brought my hand up to cup her cheek, unable to resist touching her soft skin. I brushed my callused thumb along her jaw. 'Hey.' Her eyes met mine. 'I'm sorry. I get sensitive about her.'

'Yeah, I noticed. That's the last time I try to do something nice.' Her tone was serious, but she looked up at me with that crooked mischievous smile of hers. I wanted to kiss the smirk off her gorgeous face.

'Aw, don't be that way, cupcake. Come on. Stay for dinner.'

She checked her watch. 'That could probably be arranged.'

'You got somewhere to be? Don't tell me it's another hot date with that country club schmuck.'

She chuckled. 'No, actually Peter hasn't called. It's just my mom's been hounding me about coming over for dinner. Let me step outside to call her and see if I can postpone till tomorrow night.'

'Sure. Come inside when you're done.'

Lily came tearing down the hall to show off her matching pink fingernails and toenails and the pink ceramic fairy she'd painted. It was like an explosion of pink had invaded my house—hell, my life.

'I'm gonna go put it in my room,' she announced, already heading down the hall.

Alexa returned and headed straight for me, a smile on her face. I pulled her into a hug. 'Well? Can you stay?'

She nuzzled into my neck and inhaled. 'Yeah, but I had to make a deal with my mother.'

I kissed her lips then pulled back to look at her. 'What's that?'

'I told her I was at my friend Cade's and she insisted that you join us for dinner. Are you free tomorrow?'

'Dinner? With your parents?' I held her at arms' length, looking her over. She couldn't be serious. I thought we were just having fun, but this…meeting the parents was something more, wasn't it?

Her bottom lip jutted out. 'Is that okay?'

'Ah, sure. I can probably get Sophia to come over.'

Her smile momentarily faltered at the mention of Sophia's name. 'Okay.'

Alexa helped Lily wash her hands while I set the table. I'd stopped at the neighborhood diner, and not knowing what Alexa would like, I'd picked up a burger and a grilled chicken salad for her, along with my usual burger and Lily's grilled-cheese sandwich.

Once we were all seated around the table, Alexa chose the grilled chicken salad for dinner and Lily announced she wanted salad, too. Alexa graciously shared the salad, dividing it onto two plates while I stuffed the extra food in the fridge for dinner another night.

We made small talk while we ate, Alexa and Lily both reminiscing about their girls' day. Once we finished with dinner, Alexa hopped up from her chair. 'Oh, I almost forgot. I got dessert.' She retrieved the pink bakery box from the counter.

I shook my head slowly. 'You spoil us. What'd you get?'

'Cupcakes, what else?' She grinned.

I chuckled and Lily clapped her hands, completely unaware of Alexa's nickname. I leaned back, draping an arm across the back of Alexa's chair and watched as Alexa removed a pink-frosted cupcake from the box and placed it in front of Lily, peeling off the paper cup. Lily's eyes went wide and she wasted no time biting into the enormous treat. By her enthusiasm, you'd think I never fed the poor kid. Alexa chuckled and wiped pink frosting from the tip of Lily's nose.

We watched Lily demolish her cupcake in relative silence. 'You didn't have to do all this you know.'

'I wanted to,' she returned.

I knew there was no use in arguing with her, but something about it didn't sit quite right with me. Was she here caring for Lily and hanging around me because she felt bad for us? We were not a fucking charity case for her to take pity on.

Seeming to sense my mood, Alexa dipped her index finger into the frosting of a cupcake and brought it to my mouth, her eyes sparkling with challenge. I reached out and gripped her wrist, my eyes locked on hers as I swirled my tongue gently across the pad of her finger.

Alexa let out a ragged moan. Lily giggled at the sight of us, pulling our attention back to the fact that we had an audience.

I cleared my throat, trying to regain some composure and stop the throbbing ache low in my balls. 'Do you want to show Alexa how to start your bath water while I clean up the kitchen?'

Lily hopped up and with one hand holding her walker, she grabbed for Alexa's hand with the other. 'Come on, Lexa. I'll show you where I keep the bubbles.'

Watching the two of them together had me wondering if Lily needed more a more stable female role model in her life. The thought was sobering.

I cleaned up the kitchen to the backdrop of pleasant sounds of feminine laughter and splashing water coming from down the hall. Once I was through I peeked into the bathroom, finding Lily covered in bubbles, playing with her bath toys and Alexa kneeling over the side of the tub, wiggling that fine little ass at me. I took a moment to inspect her shapely backside, the way her jeans hugged her curves and the way her shirt had ridden up, exposing the curve of her lower back. She was sexy as hell and didn't even know it. And seeing her nurturing side with Lily—hell, that just set off all kinds of alpha male in me. I wanted her.

They caught sight of me watching, and Alexa straightened, pulling her shirt down to cover the bare flesh of her back.

'Lexa, you can have a bath and use my bubbles when I'm done, if you want,' Lily said.

Alexa's eyes went wide, blush rising in her cheeks. She gave the little girl a tremulous smile. 'Oh, no thanks, sweetheart. It's okay.'

'Finish up. It's bedtime,' I growled.

They turned at the gruffness of my voice and Alexa's eyes lingered on mine. 'Come on, lets rinse you off,' she instructed, her voice just as shaky as mine.

Alexa tucked Lily into bed and met me in the living room. Without a word or a single moment of hesitation, Alexa crossed the room, and lowered herself on my lap. I cupped her ass, tugging her in closer, and kissed her. Her soft, tender kisses were messing with my head. This no longer felt like we were just fooling around. It felt like more. Much more.

Chapter 14

Alexa

Cade had turned on a movie under the ploy of us cuddling on the couch, but the way his body was pressed firmly against my backside, and he nuzzled and nibbled at my neck was a teensy bit distracting. I could feel his heartbeat against my body, and relaxed into the comfort he provided, even if it couldn't last forever.

'Where do you live, Lex?' he asked softly.

'Hm?'

He absently twirled a lock of my hair around his finger.

'Across town.' I yawned. 'Why?'

'I don't like you having to drive home late at night in the dark.' His gentle concern hung in the air around us feeling out of place, but sweet nonetheless. 'But if you stayed here… Lily would ask all kinds of questions that I'm not ready to answer.'

What he meant was, he wasn't yet ready to discuss where this relationship was heading. Were we even in relationship territory? *God, I really needed to get a grip.* 'It's fine Cade. I live in a safe building. I have underground parking and a doorman.' I didn't mention the on-site fitness center, spa and twenty-four hour concierge, knowing they were a part of my life that Cade wasn't used to.

He didn't press the issue further, but I could tell my answer hadn't satisfied him. He draped a heavy arm around my middle and tugged me in tighter against him.

'How is it possible you're still a virgin, cupcake? You're sexy as hell.'

I considered not only his question, but also my answer. It wasn't something I'd planned on. 'I went to an all-girls private school, and the few dates I had were mostly chaperones to my dances, arranged by my parents. We spent Christmases in Aspen, summers at our lake house, and I guess there just really wasn't time.'

I shifted, snuggling in closer to his warm body. 'I decided to stay nearby for college rather than moving away and finding my own path like I'd promised myself I would. And I guess I just kept right on the living in the mold my parents had created. Stupid, huh?'

'Not at all, baby. That's not what I meant.' He gave me a squeeze, holding me close. 'I know I'm not the type you usually date, but maybe…just for now…'

'Shh. Let's just go with it, Cade.' I laced my fingers with his and brought them to my lips to press a kiss to the back of his hand. He chuckled against my ear, sending a warm whisper of breath down the back of my neck.

'I can think of something I'd like you kissing better than my hand.' His voice was low and rough.

I reached behind me to feel the growing erection in his jeans and he sucked in a ragged breath. I rolled over on the narrow couch so that I was facing him. His eyes were dark and intense, and full of desire. Wordlessly, we each began unbuttoning the other's jeans while our tongues collided in a frantic kiss.

Cade yanked my jeans down my legs, taking my panties with them. I tugged his pants and boxers down just enough until I felt the warmth of his solid cock pressing against my naked belly. I grasped him in both hands, plentiful as he was, and carefully stroked him.

'Fuck that feels good.' He watched my hands work up and down, growling low in his throat. He tugged at the hem of my shirt, and I released him momentarily to lift my arms above my head, allowing him to remove the offending piece of fabric.

He hauled me on top of him so I was lying flush against his body, his tense erection nudging at my opening. We were so close, just a few millimeters more and he would be inside me. His dark gaze collided with mine and held me speechless. I rocked my hips against his, sliding his cock against my wet folds. I felt his body tense and when I opened my eyes, his were squeezed closed and he was breathing unevenly.

The sounds of soft whimpering drifted from Lily's bedroom. We pulled apart, our eyes searching each other's.

'Caden!' Lily cried out.

He hopped up, tugging on his jeans, and jogged from the room.

I sat up on the couch and pulled on my clothes. The moment was gone. I could hear Cade's low voice murmuring soothing endearments to Lily.

I slipped on my shoes and jacket. It had been a long day, and my warring emotions over Cade and fussing over Lily had left me feeling exhausted.

Cade returned a few minutes later, looking worn out.

'Is she okay?'

He rubbed the back of his neck. 'Yeah, she's fine. Just a bad dream. I put her in my bed.'

Oh.

He eyed my jacket and frowned.

'It's getting late,' I explained.

He nodded. 'Yeah, I suppose so.' He crossed the room in two easy strides and pulled me to his chest, planting a soft kiss on my mouth. 'Good night.'

'Night,' I whispered, breathless from his kiss.

He walked me to the curb and stood near the car door when I climbed inside.

'So tomorrow, right? What time?'

'Six. We'll meet in front of the Sherman Oaks Country Club.'

He shook his head. 'Damn, cupcake…'

I knew I'd conveniently left out the part about the dinner being at my parents' club. I grinned at him sweetly. 'Oh, and Cade? Wear a tie.' I closed my car door on his stunned expression and pulled away. How we went from porn-star-slash-patient to pseudo-boyfriend, I had no idea. Despite the cozy domestic day we'd shared, I couldn't forget that Cade and I came from very different walks of life, and knew that dinner with my parents would test whatever relationship we'd developed.

I spotted Cade right away. He was dressed in a white button-down shirt and navy tie, with navy slacks to match. He looked sexy as sin, but I couldn't help but notice how out of place he looked in the entryway of the hoity-toity club, his tattoo playing peek-a-boo with his shirt collar. And he must have felt it too, because his eyes darted around the parking lot, searching me out and the set of his shoulders only relaxed when his eyes met mine.

He appraised me with a sexy grin as I approached, my stiletto heels clicking against the brick walkway. He pressed a hand to my lower back once I was near and drew me close, dropping a kiss to my throat. 'You look sexy, cupcake,' he growled.

I blushed at his compliment, looking down at the fitted black dress I rarely got the chance to wear anymore. 'Thanks.' My eyes searched the parking lot and when I spotted my parents' approach I pulled away from Cade's embrace.

My mom wore a pale-blue pantsuit and my dad was in his customary Sunday attire—chinos and a navy blazer, collar unbuttoned, no tie. It was the only day of the week he went sans-tie, considering he worked nearly twenty-four seven. But I knew Cade wearing one would make the right impression.

As they approached, Cade leaned in towards my ear. 'Why did I have to wear a tie if he didn't?'

I elbowed his ribs, fixing a smile on my face as my parents approached.

A man in a suit approached from our left, tossing a set of keys into Cade's hand. 'Hey, keep it running, I'll be back in a few.'

Cade's eyes met mine, full of irritation. Oh! My confusion cleared and I realized he thought Cade was the valet.

Cade grumbled something at the man, and tossed the keys back to him just as my parents stopped beside us.

My mom and I exchanged kisses and I gave my dad a quick hug before introducing them to Cade.

They smiled at him politely and he and my dad shook hands. 'What was that?' my dad asked, tipping his head towards the guy now waiting by the curb for the actual valet.

'Just a misunderstanding,' I interjected quickly before Cade could open his mouth, and fixed a smile on my face.

This felt strange. Way strange. *Go with it, Alexa.*

My mother's eyes roamed over my dress and her mouth pinched closed. I tugged at the hem of my skirt, willing it closer to my knees. Cade noticed what I was doing and took my hand in his, giving it a firm squeeze before releasing it. I took a deep breath and trailed behind my parents into the dining room.

The hostess seated us at my parents' usual table near the windows overlooking the golf course. Seeing how fall was settling in, not many golfers were braving the course today, but for a few dedicated souls just finishing the back nine.

Cade was ever the gentlemen, seeming to have moved passed the valet mishap, and pulled out my chair before settling in his own.

He frowned at the expansive quantity of silverware at his place setting and I gave his knee a gentle squeeze underneath the table.

'Alexa's never brought a *date* to our Sunday dinners,' my mom said, suspiciously eyeing Cade.

Cade, thinking quick on his feet, grasped my hand on top of the table. 'Well I'm happy to be here.'

My mom settled back into her chair, her back still ramrod straight, but seemingly satisfied with his response.

The server came by for our drink order, beginning with Cade— he ordered a bottle of beer. I winced. We never drank at Sunday dinners. It was sort of a thing with my parents. The rest of us ordered iced tea.

When the server returned with our drinks, Cade waved away the suggestion of a pilsner glass and I thought my mother's eyes were going to pop out of her head. But when he tipped his head back and drank straight from the bottle, exposing a little section of his tattoo, my mother sucked in a gasp and gripped the table-cloth in front of her.

I wanted to go to the bathroom and hide. It wouldn't have been the first time I'd done so. The farthest stall back on the left side of the ladies' room had served as a disappearing place a few times over the years when I needed to escape my mother's meddling.

Dad finally asked the question I knew had been on his mind since meeting Cade. 'So, what do you do, Cade?'

Cade pulled back another fortifying swig of this beer before answering. 'I work construction. Roofing mostly.'

'Hmm,' my mother pursed her lips.

My dad simply nodded. 'You enjoy working with your hands? I never was much good at it. Hell, I practically have to call an electrician just to change a lightbulb.'

Cade smiled, relaxing just a bit into his chair. 'Yeah, I like seeing the tangible results of my work. I do all sorts of things, carpentry, electrical—let me know if you ever need a hand. I draw the line at plumbing, but the rest I can usually figure out.'

I'd never really heard Cade talk about his work, I realized. I liked hearing him describe it. It was the same way I felt about nursing. I liked the notion of helping to improve something, leaving it in better condition than the way I found it. Sure, my work was with people, and Cade's was with inanimate materials, but I still understood what he meant. I doubted my dad could relate, balance sheets weren't exactly exciting. But I liked that he nodded and smiled, at least trying to relate to Cade.

The waiter was soon back, taking our order. 'The prime-rib special Mr. and Mrs. Blake?'

My parents nodded in agreement. Cade handed over his menu without looking at it. 'You have burgers here?'

The waiter nodded. 'Certainly, sir.'

Without knowing what possessed me, perhaps it was the carefree chicken-wing-eating Lexa making her comeback, I followed Cade's lead. 'I'll take the burger too.'

'But you always get the prime rib—' my mother interrupted.

'I know, but I'm in the mood for a burger tonight.'

'Don't be silly, she'll have the prime rib,' my mother told the waiter.

The waiter's gaze bounced between me and my mother, seemingly unsure of who to listen to, when Cade interrupted. 'Alexa's a big girl, she knows what she wants.' The statement was laced with deeper meaning and we all knew it.

I couldn't help but smile at him before turning to the waiter. 'The burger, please. Well done with gouda cheese.'

Cade leaned back, draping his arm over the back of my chair, casually sipping his beer.

'Have you seen much of Peter, dear?' my mom asked.

Nice timing Mom.

Cade's gazed flicked to mine, clearly interested in my response.

'No, mother,' I said in a clipped tone, sending her a *drop it* glare.

The rest of the dinner passed without further drama. My dad and Cade tried to find topics to discuss, and after several false starts with 401k investments, and then politics, they finally settled on something on which they could both agree—Chicago Bears football. They were soon animatedly discussing draft picks and the quarterback's latest arrest.

My mother ate in silence, stabbing at her dinner and pushing it around her plate. My burger was delicious, and I wondered why I'd never ordered for myself before. I ate every bite and was nearly bursting from my dress by the time we left the restaurant a short while later.

Cade and I lingered in the parking lot after my parents pulled away. His pickup truck stuck out like a sore thumb in the parking lot full of luxury sedans and SUVs. My own included.

'Is Sophia watching Lily?'

'Yeah,' he replied.

'Do you have time to come over for a drink? I don't live far from here.' I liked the idea of him seeing where I lived, not to mention, I was eager to finish where we left off last night before we were interrupted by Lily's nightmare.

He sighed and ran his hands through his hair, then yanked his tie loose at the collar. 'I'd better not.'

The air around us changed. It felt stiff, cold. 'Cade?' I shifted a step closer. 'What is it?' I braced myself, ready to hear that my judgmental mother had proved too much for him and he was cutting out on me.

'I need to get home to Lily.' His eyes refused to meet mine and I knew there was something he was holding back.

I was about to tell him that Lily would be fine for an hour, but something about his stiff stance told me to not to press him. 'Oh, I suppose I could come to your place, then.'

He took a step back. 'Not tonight, Alexa.'

I frowned, and when I suddenly realized that he'd called me Alexa rather than cupcake, my stomach twisted into a painful knot. 'What's wrong?'

'Listen, Lex. You and I are fun, but we both know I can't afford the shit you're used to. Prime-rib dinners and three-hundred-dollar pedicures don't fit in to my life. This is bound to end sometime and the more time we spend together will only hurt Lily more when that happens. '

'I'm sorry, I just thought the warm soak and massage would be good for her legs.' That spa visit hadn't been about me. I'd done it with Lily in mind. His eyes widened in understanding, and a flash of guilt flickered through them.

'Regardless, you know I'm right. The disapproval was written all over your parents' faces. I didn't go to college. I don't have some fancy degree. I have responsibilities—a mortgage, and full custody of a six-year-old.'

'What was all that stuff inside about *Alexa's a big girl, she knows what she wants*?' I challenged. Sure, he had responsibilities, but when had I ever showed him I wasn't on board with Lily? And so what if he didn't have a college degree? He had a freakin' Masters in seduction.

'You're an adult. You should be able to stand up to your parents.'

'Well…I know what I want.' My tone was defiant and my eyes didn't waver from his.

He sighed and looked past me. 'That may be, but I have a little girl to take care of. She doesn't have anyone else. She has to come first. I'm sorry.'

'I know.' I understood that, I truly did.

'Are you telling me you think your parents would ever accept us dating? No. You know they wouldn't. You mom was trying to set you up with Peter while I was sitting right there.'

'I don't care.'

'I do.' His expression didn't waver. It was like someone had stomped on my chest, and I struggled for breath.

'Cade…' I reached out for his forearm, but he took a step back.

'Go on home, Alexa.'

His emotionless tone all but froze my skin and I stumbled a step back in my heels. Not wanting him to see me cry, I turned and fled for my car.

Chapter 15

Cade

Keeping my distance from Alexa was proving more difficult than I ever imagined. Every single day I had half a mind to drive up to the hospital to see her, and Lord knows I wanted to check on her, hear her voice, see how she was faring. Not to mention, during the first days of Alexa's absence, Lily drove me up a fucking wall talking about *Lexa* nonstop. I hadn't meant to lose my temper with her, but since I had, she hadn't brought up the topic of Alexa again.

Thank fucking God.

It was just like I told Alexa—I knew from the beginning things would end this way, with a certain little girl wondering where she'd gone and my heart fucking crushed because of it.

There was no denying that meeting Alexa's parents had changed things. After that exchange of words in the parking lot, we hadn't talked at all. I'd almost broken down and called her half a dozen times, but was trying like hell to give her some distance. She had to see this thing between wasn't going to work. I mean, what did she expect, that I'd win over her parents, put a ring on her finger? Of course she deserved nothing less. But the real world wasn't like one of those goddamn fairytale stories of Lily's.

After ignoring several calls from Rick, I'd finally given in, deciding it was time to do another film. I told myself this was

99

it—it would be my last one. I'd pay off Lily's outstanding bills, plus that ER visit of mine and be done with the whole thing.

I picked up my phone and dialed, knowing I only had a few minutes before Lily was due off the bus. 'Rick? Yeah, I'll do it. When and where?'

I listened as he gave me the instructions. Tomorrow. Shave in the morning. Be on location at noon.

'Done. See you then.' I ended the call. I hadn't even asked who I'd be working with. It didn't matter. I needed the money. My contract stated what I wouldn't do—the whole *gay for pay* thing—and the rest, I knew I could handle.

Once I met Lily off the bus and got her settled in with a snack and her 'toons, I grabbed a bottle of beer and took off for the garage, needing to blow off some steam by reorganizing my toolbox, or punching something. Take your pick.

It did little to relieve my tension, and ten minutes later I was stalking back inside. 'Lily?'

It was completely silent in the house. Not a good sign. I rounded the corner from the kitchen to the living room and stepped in something wet, and warm. *What the—?*

When I entered the living room, the reason for the damp carpeting became clear. Lily had maneuvered a large pot of water into the living room and dumped it onto the floor, based on the puddle I was standing in and the overturned pot in front of me.

'Lily, what in the world?' I grabbed the overturned pot, then reached down to wrench off my soaking wet socks.

I found Lily crying silently on the couch. I rushed to her. 'Baby doll? What happened?'

She sniffed, pulling her bottom lip into her mouth. 'I wanted to do a pedicure like me and Lexa did.'

That's what the pot of water had been for? To soak her feet? I hugged her to my chest. 'Shh. It's okay. It'll be okay.' Fuck. I had no training in how to deal with this. How would I handle when she started her period or wanted to go on a date? Dammit.

Just when I was starting to get on with my life and put the ache of missing Alexa behind me, life happened and landed a blow to my gut. My first instinct was to call Alexa, to beg her to come back, but I continued cleaning up the rest of the water, trying to talk myself out of it. When I couldn't hold off any longer, I pulled my phone from my pocket and dialed her number. The line rang several times before her voicemail picked up. Damn. I hung up without leaving a message. What would I say? I'm an asshole, but can you put that aside and come back? Yeah, that would work.

I dumped the wet rags into the sink as my cell phone rang. I pulled it from my pocket and the screen flashing Alexa's name sent my heart jumping. Alexa.

'Cupcake?'

She laughed nervously, all warm and feminine. God, I'd needed to hear that laugh. My tense shoulders instantly eased and I sank down into a chair at the kitchen table.

'Cade?' her voice was guarded. 'I saw you called.'

I hated hearing her so formal and down to business. 'Yeah, it's just…Lily…she's been pretty torn up since you left.'

'Lily has?' she questioned, her voice tinged with a touch of sarcasm.

'Yeah,' I said, losing my nerve.

'Well, let's clear something up. I didn't *leave*, I was pushed away. There's a difference, you know.'

'I know,' I said sheepishly.

She let out an exasperated sigh. 'Now tell me what happened with Lily.'

I explained the upturned pot of water on my floor and the fact that Lily was currently camped out on the couch in one of my old T-shirts, eating a bowl of ice cream. Before dinner. Just to quiet her sobs about the spilled water.

'I'll be over in ten minutes,' Alexa said.

'Thank you, cupcake.'

'Let me clarify one thing,' she snapped, her voice laced with anger, 'I'm coming for Lily. Not you.' And with that she hung up. *Damn.*

Having Alexa on her way made everything feel lighter, feel right somehow. Even if she was only coming for Lily, the spilled water and the soaking wet carpeting, none of which bothered me anymore. I headed into my room to change my wet clothes and wait for Alexa to arrive.

Alexa's arrival was met with squeals of laughter and Lily grabbing for her walker to race to greet her at the front door. I stood back and watched Alexa scoop her up in a hug. Alexa was positively glowing. She was more beautiful than my memory could have processed. Her hair was swept up into a loose ponytail, several tendrils escaping to frame her face and she was dressed casually in jeans and a fitted pink top. She looked good enough to eat. My very own cupcake.

But Alexa was all business, taking care of Lily and ignoring me completely. I'd never felt awkward in my own house, but it sure as shit did now. She lifted Lily to her hip, cradling and rocking her. 'Sh,' Alexa whispered. 'I'm here.'

Hearing Lily ask her in between sobbing hiccups why she hasn't been around tugged at my heart.

Once Lily was calmed and quieted, Alexa strode into the kitchen, grabbed her purse from the kitchen table and started for the door.

I reached for her hand, but she shrugged herself free from my grasp.

'Please, Lex. Will you stay?'

Her eyes met mine, full of questions. 'For you or for Lily?'

I swallowed. 'For me.' I took her hand again, noticing that she no longer fought me, yet her hand remained limp in mine. I gave it a squeeze.

'I recall you saying—' Alexa started.

'I know what I said, but I'm an idiot, okay?'

'Yes, you are,' she agreed. I could hear the smile in her voice, even if her face remained impassive.

'So will you stay? I'll even cook for you. It won't be prime rib, but...'

She chuckled. 'I suppose I could eat.'

'Come on. I've got two pretty ladies to feed.' I set Lily down in a dining room chair. 'What do you say, scrambled eggs?'

She nodded and settled into her seat, and Alexa reluctantly joined me in the kitchen.

'Eggs? For dinner?' Alexa questioned, her tone one of surprise.

'What do you have against eggs?'

'Nothing,' she back-peddled. 'I've just never had scrambled eggs for dinner.'

'Hey, you try cooking to please the palate of both an eighty-year-old and a three-year-old. I'd like to see what you come up with.'

She placed her hand on my cheek and held my eyes with hers as if to acknowledge all I'd been through. I smiled at her gentle concern, and after a moment she dropped her hand and stepped aside to allow me room to work. I removed a carton of eggs and a package of shredded cheese from the fridge and got to work.

I hadn't explained the whole story to her, and didn't plan to. That year I lost my grandmother was hard enough—she'd basically raised me. But couple that with my parents dropping off Lily, still unable to walk at age three because they hadn't invested the time or money into her care, and my grandfather's failing health...and yeah, life had been hell that year.

The truth was, none of us liked my attempts at cooking that first year, but rather than starve, we made it work. And a carton of eggs was cheap. Of course, those had been the days when we were still surviving off my grandfather's meager social security checks, before he passed away in his sleep one night and I started working full time.

Gosh, it seemed like so long ago. Now I took care of myself and Lily almost on auto-pilot, but back then, it had literally seemed an impossible feat.

After dinner, Alexa and I settled on Lily's bed while she read us a story. Even though the story she'd selected was quite a bit above her reading level, I'd read it to her so many times she had it memorized nearly word for word. My eyes drifted along Alexa's outstretched form, her arm thrown over Lily's shoulders as they huddled together on the pillow, rosy cheeks and eyes glued to the book they read from. My gaze followed the length of Alexa's lean, denim-clad legs down to her cotton-candy-pink polished toes. I ran my fingertips lightly over the arch of her bare foot and her eyes caught mine. I knew we were both anticipating being alone tonight. I also knew I had some groveling to do.

Once Lily was tucked in for the night, Alexa and I crept from the room. She started off down the hall, but my hands on her waist stopped her. I pulled her up against my chest. 'I thought we'd go in my room tonight.'

Her eyes darted up to mine, trying to understand my meaning. She blinked up at me with blue eyes widening in surprise, trusting me, following me wherever I might lead her. I took her hand and led her inside my darkened bedroom. Not bothering to turn on a light—it'd only reveal a large messy bed, and a single dresser in the corner anyhow—I gently steered her towards my bed. When I felt the backs of her legs bump against the mattress, I gave her shoulders a gentle nudge and she fell backwards, giggling as she hit the bed and tugging me down on top of her.

My lips sought out hers in the darkness, my body needing to be close to her in every way possible. Our limbs were a tangled heap in the center of the bed, though I tried to keep my weight from crushing her. I couldn't believe I'd been stupid enough to push her away. If by some small miracle this angel thought I was good enough for her, I was hers. Body and soul.

'Hey, I almost forgot. I got something for you.' I disentangled myself from her, felt my way to my dresser and located what I was looking for. 'Where's your purse?'

'You can give it to me.'

'Not right now. I'll just tuck it inside your bag for later.'

'Okay. My purse is on the couch.'

'Be right back.' I jogged down the hallway, depositing the canister into her bag before rejoining her.

She'd tugged down the blankets and was resting in the center of the bed when I returned. Once I located her, she cuddled against my chest, her head tucked under my chin as if this spot was designed solely for her. Hell, maybe it was.

She reached one hand under my T-shirt and soothed me with gentle caresses I didn't deserve. Her fingers worked away all the tension in my neck and shoulders. 'It's all going to be okay with Lily, you know. You're doing the best you can,' she whispered.

Hearing her approval of my efforts with Lily was a shock to my system. It was something I never heard from anyone, least of all myself. There was always more to do, more to worry about, more I should have been doing.

Alexa's presence in our lives was proof of that. But then again, she was filling a void I couldn't. Providing a woman's touch. And seeing the joy she brought to Lily, I wasn't about to rob Lily of that. But having Alexa acknowledge my efforts, working to calm my fears, set off something inside me and my heart squeezed in my chest. I knew I didn't deserve a woman this pure and perfect, but damn if I didn't want to keep her.

'Thank you,' I said, simply.

'I hated how we left things…in that parking lot,' she breathed against my skin.

'Shh.' I kissed away her fears, brushing her hair back from her face. 'That was my fault. Will you forgive me?'

'Hmm. That'd be too easy. You might need some reminders about how good we are together.'

I pressed a kiss to her forehead, her sweet scent rushing over me. 'I know I'm not the type you take home to Mommy and Daddy, and that never bothered me before now, but dammit Alexa. I'm sorry…' Even if I got to be the first one inside her, the first to fuck her, would it even be enough? Would I be okay with the fact that sooner or later some prick with a nice car and an office job would come along and put a ring on her finger? Fuck, I couldn't think like that. It was what she deserved. But I'd take every second I could get with her until then.

She pushed against my chest, wanting space and I rolled off of her. In the moonlight, I could just make out her silhouette as she sat back on her heels and lifted her shirt off over her head, thrusting her tits out. All the blood rushed to my groin and I bit back a groan. I swallowed, and pulled in a ragged breath. She was fucking perfection.

She pressed a few soft kisses on my throat and my chest, and rocked her hips against mine. Everything felt different with her. Sure, I was horny as hell, but it was more than that, too. There was nothing meaningless about this. With each soft cry I elicited from her, each time her gaze met mine, I was falling deeper and deeper. But I hadn't asked her to be part of my life because I knew it wasn't realistic. I'd been around the block, seen how things worked and wouldn't put Lily through that. I closed my eyes and tried to just enjoy the time I had with her.

I reached behind her and unclasped her bra, needing to taste her. Hell, I'd give my left nut for a taste. I planted several openmouthed kisses on each bare breast. She thrust her chest out, angling herself closer to my mouth. 'Don't tease me, cupcake. Not if you're not ready for this…' My voice was coarse, and my tone more menacing than I intended, but Alexa rose on her knees in the center of the bed and began unbuttoning her jeans, slowly sliding them down her hips, wiggling her fine little ass.

'The panties too,' I growled.

She slid her fingers under the elastic and tugged the panties down her legs, sending them over the side of the bed along with her jeans.

Once she was completely undressed, I tugged off my own T-shirt and yanked down my jeans, tossing them to the floor. 'Come here.' I eased her down onto her back, and spread her knees until her legs fell apart as wide as they would go, before leaning forward to taste her.

When my mouth met her flesh, her head dropped back against the pillow and she let out a low moan. I circled her clit with my tongue, teasing and sucking the delicate flesh into my mouth while she writhed underneath me. Her hips wouldn't remain still, lifting to meet my mouth as if they had a mind of their own, and I had to grip her waist to keep hold her steady. I could do this all day, but it wasn't long before she was balling the comforter in her fists and crying out my name as her release crashed over her.

I crawled up her body and held her against my chest, where she promptly nestled herself in again. 'Am I forgiven yet?' I whispered into her hair.

She sighed contentedly and patted my back. 'Mm-hmm.'

I chuckled.

Tossing aside the fact that I had a throbbing erection, I would have lain there all night just holding her, doing my best to win her over. But after a few minutes Alexa's breathing had returned to normal and she climbed on top of me, straddling my lap. The feel of her wet heat pressed against my erection sent my heart rate skyrocketing. I wanted her. Fuck, I needed her.

'You can't keep sliding that sweet pussy along my cock, sweetheart, unless you're ready for me to bury it deep inside you.'

She let out a soft whimper.

I gripped her upper arms, hard enough so she knew I was serious but not hard enough to hurt, and hauled her off me. 'I'm not going to be able to control myself with you cupcake, and I don't want to hurt you.'

'Cade, please. Inside me...' she whispered.

Aw hell, hearing her beg for it just about undid me. Did she know what she was asking me? 'Are you sure? Your first time should be with someone important, doll.'

Her answer was determined. 'I know.'

My heart spasmed again. I wanted to make her mine. 'You sure you're ready for this?'

'Yes,' she breathed, her voice raspy with need.

I planted a soft kiss on her mouth, and felt her shudder when my erection pressed against her hip. I blindly reached over to my nightstand, unwilling to break the kiss and found the foil packet I was looking for. Within seconds I had rolled on the condom, and once the familiar scent of latex hung in the air, my dick had a mind of its own, nudging against Alexa's belly as if it was seeking entrance. I knew I needed to slow myself down, but her tiny whimpers and the way she rocked her hips against mine were wearing at my patience.

I brought a hand between us to position myself between her legs and eased forward, nudging the head of my cock against her entrance, bracing myself above her. Alexa gripped my biceps as I pushed forward just slightly. She sucked in a breath and held it, biting her lip.

'Are you okay?'

I felt her nod.

I brushed her hair back from her face and dropped a kiss on her forehead as I pushed forward again. The pressure of her warm channel squeezing me was almost unbearable. I pulled back and thrust forward a third time, allowing myself to slide just a little deeper inside. I watched Alexa's expression change as I began to fill her. She was beautiful to watch—the little gasps escaping her parted lips, and her pink flushed cheeks.

When I pushed inside farther, unable to hold off from feeling the friction of our bodies any longer, Alexa released a soft cry that was tinged with both pleasure and pain.

'Am I hurting you?'

She squeezed her eyes closed and shook her head. 'Just keep going,' she instructed.

God she was so tight, my dick felt like it was being strangled. 'Holy fuck, cupcake, this has to be hurting you. Tell me if you want me to stop.'

Her only response was a series of tiny whimpers. Her eyes were squeezed closed—in pleasure or pain, I didn't know. 'Just go slow, okay?'

A surge to protect her, despite the massive case of blue balls awaiting me, swelled in my gut, and I pulled out completely, sitting back on the bed.

'Cade?' She reached for me. 'Why'd you stop?'

'Because I was hurting you.'

'So?' Her expression was one of genuine confusion. 'I knew it would hurt the first time, but I still want to…' She trailed her hand along my abs, reaching lower.

I removed her hand and pulled her body close to mine. She crawled into my lap, wrapping her arms and legs around me and I cradled her body to mine. She planted insistent kisses along the column of my neck and over my tattoo.

'Fuck, I want you, baby. Are you sure about this?'

'God yes,' she moaned.

I brought my hand to my mouth, applying saliva to my finger-tips and reached between us to rub the wetness on the head of my cock. Alexa was still soaking wet, but maybe this would help ease my entrance just enough. 'Come here, baby. Lower yourself down on me. You'll control the pressure. Only take what you can handle.' I positioned myself at her entrance, and Alexa immediately began pushing herself down on me. I bit back a string of curse words. She gripped my shoulders, her nails biting into my skin, and I cupped the globes of her ass, holding her steady.

'Cade,' she moaned, sending a spark of pleasure through my gut, hitting me straight in the balls. I wanted to unleash, to pound into her tight pussy again and again, but I held back, holding myself steady while she raised and lowered herself in tiny increments as she adjusted to my size.

Once I was fully buried in her, she threw her head back and let out a coarse moan. She opened her eyes and met mine, her pouty mouth curving into a mischievous grin. It felt amazing being buried in her sweet body, but I needed her to move or I was going to fucking explode.

Finally she began to rock her hips against mine. 'Cade, oh God.' She kissed me distractedly, her open mouth sucking and nipping at mine. I wasn't any more coordinated than she was, content for our lips to brush as I breathed against her mouth and mumbled endearments to her lips. All my focus was centered on holding onto her tight little ass while she plunged up and down on me.

She rode me faster, her chest grazing mine as she moved. 'Yeah, that's it sweetheart. Oh fuck, just like that, baby.' Knowing my self-control wasn't going to last, I reached a hand between us and rubbed the pad of my thumb over her swollen bud, sweeping circles around it. She ground her hips into mine, crying out my name.

'Are you close, baby?' I nipped at her lips, increasing the pressure on her clit and lifting my hips to meet her thrusts, unable to hold back any longer.

'Cade. I'm going to come.'

A rush of pride swelled within me and I held on as she pumped herself up and down my cock, moaning and whimpering in a sexy tumble of incoherent words, until I felt a rush of wetness as she came against me. The friction of her tight walls as she squeezed and spasmed around me sent me over the edge and I groaned out my own release, spilling myself inside her.

Chapter 16

Alexa

'Hey, sleepyhead.' Cade pressed a kiss to my forehead, and a lazy smile crossed my lips, remembering where I was—warm and cozy in Cade's bed. I opened my eyes to find his sleepy gaze inches from mine. His alarm sounded from the dresser and Cade hopped out of bed, still completely nude, to silence it.

I stretched and rolled over, taking the warmth of his vacated spot. It smelled of him—a hint of spicy cologne and the rest just his own masculine scent. *Him.* I was decidedly sore and dressed in one of Cade's T-shirt that I didn't recall putting on.

'Mmm.' I reached for him. 'Come back.'

Cade turned to face me, his morning erection greeting me as he sat on the edge of the bed next to me. He pressed a quick kiss to my mouth. 'Last night was amazing,' he murmured.

I stretched seductively, pulling the T-shirt over my head and dropping it on the floor. 'Come back to bed.'

His eyes roamed my body, and he grinned at what he saw. He traced a fingertip along my belly, circling my hipbone. 'Aren't you sore, baby?'

'Just a little. You might have to kiss it and make it all better.' I smirked seductively, trying my best attempt at dirty talk.

'I better not…I've gotta work today.'

What did that have to do with…? 'At the construction site?'

112

He looked down, tucking the edge of the blanket around me. 'Ah, no. Actually I have a film shoot today.'

I shot up in bed, tugging the sheet over my naked chest, all inhibitions of the night before gone at the mention of him... *working*. Especially when said work involved his sleeping with another woman. 'I didn't think you were still doing that. And especially after last night...' *Shit*. I was going to cry. Right here, naked in his bed and still sore from our lovemaking. I pulled in a breath to steady myself.

'Don't look at me like that. You knew what I did the first night we met.' Cade slipped into a pair of jeans, forgoing even boxers. I hated the thought that someone other than me would unwrap that package later. I couldn't share him. Sharing him with Lily was one thing, a very different thing, but certainly not something like this. God, how had I been stupid enough to think that a having a porn star for a boyfriend was a good idea?

'But after last night...' Things changed for me. Completely. But if the morning after being inside me he could go off and do the same thing to another woman without a passing thought, clearly my feelings were more one-sided than I'd believed. Sex didn't hold the same importance to him as it did to me. And I could never be with someone that didn't understand and appreciate the intimacy we'd shared. Sure I might've joked in the beginning about losing my virginity, but we both knew better. I was falling for Cade. Had fallen. Hard. And he'd taken the gift of my virginity without understanding that he now held my heart in his hands.

'Cade?'

'I'm sorry, but I've got to do this, cupcake.'

I threw the covers off and leapt from the bed. *Don't cupcake me...*

'Alexa...talk to me. What's wrong?'

I spun around, facing him. 'What's wrong? You're seriously asking me what's wrong?' I was not having this conversation while naked. I jerked on my clothes, feeling close to violence that if he so much as tried to lay one finger on me, I'd annihilate him. If he didn't know what was wrong, there was no use talking to him at all. 'So just like that, you're going to…go off and do *that* today?'

He hung his head, apparently at a loss for words.

'Don't call me.' I stomped out of his room, grabbing my purse and keys on the way, and tore out of his house to my waiting car as quickly as I could. I said a silent prayer of thanks for the pickup on my X5, the law be damned. I'd like to see anyone try to pull me over. I'd castrate a police officer before I let anyone stand in the way of me crawling into my bed. Through tear-filled eyes, I dialed MacKenzie.

''Ello?' she groaned sleepily.

'Kenzie, I need you. Now.' I sniffed, wiping my cheeks with the back of my hand. 'And bring Jell-O shots.'

She hesitated, bed springs creaking in the background. 'It's seven in the morning.'

'I know. But it's an emergency.' I wiped the tears freely streaming down my cheeks and sucked in a deep breath. 'I slept with Cade last night. And things went to shit this morning.'

'Oh, crap. Okay, hang in there, I'm on my way.' I heard rustling in the background as MacKenzie sprang into action, just like I knew she would.

'Bring vodka, too.'

'On it.'

Chapter 17

Cade

I moved through my morning in a haze, still stunned over the turn of events. How did Alexa not understand that what had happened with *us* was real, and that this was just my job? She obviously didn't trust me like I would need her to if we were going to make anything of us.

Alexa hadn't even given me a chance to explain, she'd just jumped to conclusions and stormed out on me. I hadn't bothered to stop her. The disgust and judgment written all over her face told me what I'd known deep down all along—I would never be good enough for her. She would never be able to comprehend that sometimes there were things in life that you didn't want to do, but had to do to take care of your family. And Lily was my family. I'd do anything for her. Life wasn't all fucking sunshine and rainbows. Real life was hard. I was doing what needed to be done. Period. She said she understood my responsibilities regarding caring for Lily, but when it came down to it, she bailed. End of story.

After getting Lily off to school, I took a lengthy shower, shaved my chest and groin, and then got dressed and made sure to stretch. I recalled from my previous shoot that three hours of sex will make you sore in the oddest places.

When I arrived at the set, the model I was going to be working with was already there, getting her hair and makeup done. She certainly didn't fit the porn-star image. Her looks were the epitome of the sweet girl next door. She had wavy, shoulder-length brown hair, big brown eyes and was more cute than sexy.

I went up to introduce myself. 'Hey, I'm Cade, er, I mean Sebastian.'

She smiled warmly. 'Hi. I'm Jill, but you can call me Britney.'

'Got it. Nice to meet you.' I returned her smile. At least she seemed like she'd be easy to work with, which was nice. I didn't need any more drama today. She turned back to the makeup artist to finish up, and I went to find Rick.

Today's shoot was relatively straightforward. We'd start in the opulent master bathroom, where I'd find Britney taking a bubble bath, and after spending a few minutes kissing and helping to wash her, I'd lift her from the tub and carry her into the bedroom where we'd finish out the scene.

Once I knew the setup, I got rubbed down with bronzer, and then waited for my cue from Rick. Once Britney was relaxing in the Jacuzzi tub, I sauntered in, barefoot, dressed in just a pair of jeans. We shared a few tender kisses, and I rubbed her shoulders and neck, before moving on to her breasts. Then they captured a shot of me helping her from the tub before calling cut.

We picked things up again once we were on the bed, and I was soon buried deep inside Britney. But once inside her, I couldn't escape my thoughts about the previous night with Alexa. She was so soft, so trusting that I wouldn't hurt her. Being with Britney was the complete opposite. She thrust her hips to match my strides and begged me to fuck her faster. A deep, nagging feeling boiled up, urging me on and I relented, driving into her hard and fast, chasing relief from the fire raging inside me.

Realizing I didn't have to be careful with Britney, I didn't hold back. I plowed into her until she stopped asking for it harder and started a litany of tiny whimpers. The sound of Britney's whimpers reminded me of Alexa. And holding the image of Alexa's face in my mind, I finished. But even with my release, relief didn't come.

Ian arrived just as the game was about to start.

He scanned my coffee table and gestured to the six-pack of beer and takeout pizza box with a frown. 'Hey man, where are the wings?'

I shook my head. 'Not in the mood.' It would remind me too much of Alexa. Damn, watching her sweet mouth tear the meat off the bone and her pink tongue darting out to catch a drip of barbeque sauce…no, there would be no wings tonight.

He sank to the couch, grabbing a beer.

'Have you been working much?' We both knew he wasn't asking about construction. We typically kept a *don't ask, don't tell* policy when it came to me dabbling in porn, but I'd let it slip that Alexa had left me over it, and that was why I'd been so miserable.

'Nope. I paid off the bills I needed to, and now I'm keeping myself out of all that shit.'

He nodded, sipping his beer. 'And Alexa?'

I pulled my mouth into a tight line and shook my head.

'Still? Damn you're stubborn.'

I drained my bottle and reached for a fresh beer, keeping my eyes glued to the play. 'How am I stubborn?'

'Because you're telling me you're not doing porn anymore… and the reason Alexa left you was because you were doing porn…'

'Yeah, I guess so,' I growled, picking at the label on my bottle.

'And do you not see how stupid that logic is?' Ian shook his head. 'Go after her, bro. Quit being a fucking pussy.'

'Drop it, man. It would never work between us anyways.' *Would it?*

Chapter 18

Alexa

MacKenzie and I were sitting in my living room with two wine glasses on the coffee table and a bottle of Merlot between us. It had been a long week. I woke each morning with thoughts of Cade and Lily swirling in my head and went to bed each night with tears in my eyes. I missed them both fiercely, though I'd never admit that to Cade. What he'd done was unforgiveable. He'd strung me along, pretending to be this amazing guy—he met my parents for heaven's sake—but worst of all, he'd captured my heart. It was exactly what MacKenzie had warned me about. Thank God there was no *I told you so*. She just listened when I needed to vent, and kept quiet when I didn't want to talk, and she'd come over every night this past week to distract me.

After a few glasses of wine MacKenzie had begun trying to pump me for information about how Cade was in bed.

I wasn't giving anything away.

She took another sip of her wine, cocking a hand on her hip. 'Hell, I could be seven months pregnant with another man's baby and I'd still want a piece of him.'

'Not helping.' I frowned at her.

She held up her hands. 'Sorry, but that's the truth. Listen, sweetie, you had your fun. Maybe just chalk it up to getting some experience under your belt, and let the rest go.'

What she didn't understand was that it wasn't that easy. It wasn't just Cade that had stolen my heart, it was sweet Lily too. They were a package deal in my mind.

I heard a knock at the door, and then the key turning. It had to be Tyson letting himself in.

MacKenzie perked up at the sound. 'You better have pizza!' she called.

We both giggled. We'd called him thirty minutes ago begging him to bring us a pizza. Extra cheese, extra pepperoni.

Tyson entered the living room, a pizza box balanced on his hand. 'My ladies.' He placed it on the coffee table between us.

'Ty, you are the best,' I said, reaching toward him for a one-armed hug.

'No problem. I'll go get some plates and napkins.' He headed into the kitchen while MacKenzie and I opened the lid and inhaled the amazing aroma emanating from the box. I was glad to see there wasn't any lingering awkwardness between Ty and I. I knew he was still pissed over my little fling with Cade, but for now, he was being civil about it.

'Get yourself a glass,' I called in to Ty.

'And bring another bottle of wine!' MacKenzie added.

Without waiting for the plates, MacKenzie and I each grabbed a slice.

After finishing off the large pizza and three bottles of wine we decided to call it a night. I walked them to the door and grabbed for my wallet to pay Ty back for the pizza. I handed Ty a few bills before hugging them both goodnight.

When I returned my wallet to my purse, my hand bumped something cool and firm. *What the—?*

I pulled the black bottle from my purse and I held it up to inspect. 'The Guardian?' I read the side. 'What the hell is this?'

It appeared to be pepper spray. Where in the world...? Oh my gosh. Cade. He'd stuffed something into my purse that night, saying he'd gotten me a gift. I'd forgotten all about it.

I set the offending object on my kitchen island and paced the room. Why did he get me that? Why did he try to act like he cared when he so obviously didn't?

Without waiting for logic to set in, I grabbed my cell phone and dialed his number. It'd been over a week since *the incident*, but my newfound liquid courage had provided the fuel needed to make the call.

Despite the late hour, he answered on the first ring.

'What the hell do you think you're doing?'

His low chuckle washed over me, making my insides tremble. 'Are you drunk, cupcake?'

Oh, so I was cupcake again? 'No!' *Yes.*

'Then you're going to have to explain what the hell you're referring to. I'm at a loss here, doll.'

He needed to cut the sweet nicknames out. *Right fucking now.* 'This spray you snuck in my purse.'

'It's just mace. I didn't want to worry about you alone and helpless on your own. Consider it a gift.'

I sucked in a deep breath. 'Well for your information, I already have mace. My dad gave me a canister of it a few years ago. It's somewhere in my kitchen. And I'm not alone. I've started seeing Peter again.' Or at least I would, when I returned his phone call.

Cade hesitated a moment, the silence erecting a wall between us. 'That was fast. Good for you. But your mace isn't going to be much of a help stuck inside some drawer and if it's a few years old, it's probably expired. Besides, the one I got you is the best one on the market. Keep it in your purse, cupcake.'

I rolled my eyes and jammed the canister back inside my purse. Bringing up Peter's name didn't have quite the response I'd hoped for. 'I've gotta go.' I hit End on my cell, but not before I heard his rich chuckle vibrate through the speaker. *Bastard.*

I buried my face in my hands, fighting back tears. God, getting over Cade was going to be so much harder than I ever imagined.

The next morning, a pounding headache and the ache of hearing his voice were my only reminders of last night's activities. I'd been stupid to call him, but it obviously didn't change anything between us. Then again, what had I expected to happen? For him to beg for me to come back? Not likely. But now that I had opened up contact, I couldn't get my mind off Cade no matter what I tried. A long jog around my neighborhood with music blasting loud enough to jar all thoughts from my skull followed by a long hot shower, and then treating myself to my favorite sushi place for lunch. None of it worked. When I got home from my lunch date for one, I was even more down than I was before. Maybe there would always be some strange connection to Cade I would always feel because he was the first guy I really cared about, and the guy I gave my virginity to. Maybe I'd just need to get used to living with the ever-present achy feeling in my chest. God, what a depressing thought.

I picked up my phone and called Peter, reluctantly agreeing to another date just to get my mind off Cade, and then flopped back against my couch.

My laptop sitting next to me gave me an idea. A very, *very* bad idea.

I clicked a link titled Sebastian and Britney. As I waited for the video to load, butterflies took flight inside my stomach.

The girl was pretty. She looked sweet and normal. I watched Cade's latest video—the one he'd probably made after waking up in bed with me—with tears streaming down my cheeks. What he did wasn't a simple screw up. It was an unforgiveable mistake that was on the Internet for everyone and their brother to see. And there could be no denying it was him, especially with such a unique tattoo crawling up his shoulder.

I watched in horror as he placed her in the center of the bed and began kissing her. When he moved between her thighs to taste her, my stomach knotted and I forced my eyes closed. I knew it was a bad idea to watch this, to see it with my own eyes, knowing it would likely be burned into my brain forever, but somehow I couldn't stop. I fast forwarded the video until they were fully intertwined, needing to see if his love-making with her was anything like it was with me.

What I saw made my jaw hit the floor. His strokes into her were hard and fast. He'd been holding part of himself back with me, that much was clear. I couldn't believe that at one time watching Cade's video had turned me on—now it just pissed me off. The close-up of him sliding in and out of her almost made me vomit. I slammed my laptop closed and ran from the room. I collapsed in a heap in the center of my bed and sobbed, hugging a pillow to my chest, begging the pain to go away. But all I saw when I closed my eyes was Cade's lustful expression as he drove into her.

'Oh, hell no. I will cut a bitch.' MacKenzie sauntered across the bar to where a group of girls were climbing onto the barstools we'd been waiting twenty minutes to occupy.

'It's fine, Kenz.' I gripped her elbow, pulling her back from the scene she was about to create. 'We'll find another table.' *Or we could just go home.* After the second week of my moping, MacKenzie and Ty decided to host an intervention. It began with some pre-drinks at my apartment, and had moved on to some crowded bar.

'No. We need to find a table near the pool tables.'

I had no idea what was up with her insistence—none of us played pool. 'Those people are leaving.' I pointed across the room.

'Sweet!' MacKenzie practically sprinted, elbowing people out of her way as she crossed the room.

Jeez. I didn't know what had gotten into her, but Tyson and I dutifully followed. I climbed up on the stool and placed my purse on the tabletop. It felt good to give my feet a break. Why I'd decided to wear heels tonight was beyond me, especially when all I felt like doing was lying in bed in my pajamas. After ordering another round of drinks, Tyson let out a groan.

'What now?' I turned in the direction he was looking, but his hands gripped either side of my face, stopping me.

'No, Lex. Don't look.'

What in the world?

I removed his hands from my face and spun in the direction he and MacKenzie were both staring.

Oh.

Cade was here.

A mix of emotions rushed through me at the sight of him—everything from anger, to resentment, to desire. Damn traitorous body.

Cade and a male friend were racking a set of balls in the center of one of the pool tables and keeping up an easy banter between them.

I hated that his presence alone had the power stop my breathing and send my heart lurching in my chest, like my body knew we were sharing the same oxygen and was rebelling against the idea.

Cade was laughing, but when he looked up and caught my eyes his smile fell. I wondered if he'd come over and talk to me, and then wondered how I would feel if he didn't. He said something to his friend, whose gaze cut to mine. He cracked the slightest smile, as if in understanding, and shoved Cade in my direction. Refusing to budge, Cade remained planted near the pool table, his eyes looking anywhere but at me.

MacKenzie, smiling confidently, straightened in her chair. 'Now everyone, let's not freak out. So Cade's here. He happens to be at the same bar as us. It's no big deal.'

'You little sneak! You didn't!' MacKenzie's utter lack of surprise at seeing Cade tipped me off. She'd set this up.

Tyson glanced anxiously between us, unaware of what he had missed.

'It wasn't your place to interfere. God, did you tell him I wanted to see him?' I buried my face in my hands.

MacKenzie leaned closer, placing her hand on my arm. 'Of course not. Listen, you need to man up. I just told him we'd be here tonight, and if he wanted to see you, if he still had any feelings for you at all, he should show up around nine in the billiards room.'

'You idiot, Kenz. It doesn't work this way. I need my distance…' Hell, I needed to never think of him again, not that that was working.

Ty patted my back. I knew this was all MacKenzie's doing, so I couldn't be mad at him. 'Fine. He's here. Then I'm leaving.' I grabbed for my purse.

'No, Lex. If you leave, it'll be like announcing that you can't handle being around him.'

'I can't. That's the point.'

She gave my hand a squeeze. 'He doesn't need to know that. Don't let him drive you away. Don't let him win. You're stronger than that.'

I sighed and set my purse back down. 'Fine. Then I'm getting intoxicated.'

'Now that I can work with.' MacKenzie smiled and signaled the waitress for a round of shots to go with our other drinks.

After several rounds of drinks and watching Cade from the corner of my eye, I noticed he was approaching our table.

Oh crap. Act normal, act normal!

Ty fixed a hand on my forearm. 'Don't, Lex. Not again, not with him.' His eyes pleaded with me.

Cade sauntered up, offered a friendly nod to MacKenzie, narrowed his eyes at Tyson, then turned his gaze on me.

'Maybe we should give you guys a minute to talk,' MacKenzie squeaked, rising from her barstool and shooting Ty a *let's go* look. 'I'll go keep your sexy friend company.' She glanced in the direction of Cade's dark-haired, muscular-as-hell friend standing alone at the pool table, drinking a beer. 'What's his name?'

'Ian,' Cade answered, his eyes not wavering from mine. Once my friends had all but deserted me, Cade moved in a step closer. 'How have you been?' He scrubbed a hand over the back of his neck.

That was a dumb question. But I wasn't about to admit how I'd fallen apart over our split. 'Fine. You?'

His eyes narrowed, searching mine. I knew he could see right through my hollow answers, but I didn't care. I wouldn't give him the satisfaction of letting him know how much I missed him. 'I've been better,' he admitted.

I shook my head, surprising myself by laughing. The giggle bubbled up from my throat and escaped, despite my intentions to play things cool. 'You're a piece of work, you know that? Sex means something to me. It might not to you, but…' I waved him away. 'Just leave me alone. I don't want to talk to you.'

He caught my wrist and held it. 'Let me explain something to you, cupcake.' He'd never pronounced my nickname with such venom, and I hated to admit that it stung. He leaned in closer to my face, just inches away from me. 'Sex for money has no emotion. It's like being at work—it's hard, you're tired, sweaty, you just want to finish, but you can't. You have to keep faking the whole fucking act until some asswipe director tells you to come. On command. You try doing that with lighting techs shining bright lights in your face, and a sound guy with beer belly holding a microphone over you while sporting a fucking erection—it's not all that much fun. Believe me. I'm sure as shit not proud of it. But you know I'd do anything for that little girl.'

'Lily? What does that have to do with Lily? If you're twisted enough turn this into some chivalrous act to protect your little sister, you're more deranged than I thought.' He still had my wrist in his grip, and I pulled it away from him. 'Let me go,' I ground out through gritted teeth. I slid from my stool and escaped to the bathroom.

Chapter 19

Cade

Damn, just the sight of her and my resolve was weakening. I was two seconds away from dragging her off caveman-style to make her tell me what was on her mind when she cut out on me.

Alexa's genuine surprise at seeing me told me that MacKenzie had lied. Dammit. I couldn't believe I'd fallen for that shit about Alexa being miserable without me. She didn't look miserable, she looked gorgeous. So much so it was like a kick to the gut, ripping the air form my lungs. But hearing the bitterness in her words, seeing the glaring anger in her eyes was like a stark warning to stay the fuck away from her. Too bad I couldn't.

Her absence left an aching hole in me and I wasn't afraid to admit it. Now if I could just think of a way to convince her that I worth her time. But getting her to trust me again? The death glare she shot me in the bar told me I was going to have an uphill battle. But she was worth it. She was everything. Damn, I sounded like some lovesick fool.

As I watched her disappear into the restroom, my mind briefly registered that her jeans were low enough to expose a toned strip of lower back, and the fabric hugged the curves of her ass. Hell, lesser men would have buckled by now.

I stalked off to the restroom after her. I reminded myself that she'd been the one to storm off that morning—I doubted anything

I could have said would have made a difference, but tonight she was running again and I had to try.

I pushed open the door to the ladies' room to find it empty. But I could hear soft sobs coming from the stall at the end of the row.

'Lexa?' I tapped softly on the door. 'Can we start over? Talk about that morning you left?'

She sniffed. 'There's nothing to talk about, Cade. The damage is done.'

My shoulders sagged. Could this thing between us really be damaged beyond repair? God, I hoped not.

A group of girls pushed their way inside the restroom, giggling and chattering. 'Hey, you can't be in here,' one of them called. 'You have two seconds to get out.'

I knocked on Alexa's door more insistently. 'Come on, let me in.'

Silence.

'Cupcake?' I pled, my voice softening.

The lock turned. I didn't wait for her to open the door. I pushed it aside and was suddenly face-to-face with her in the tiny stall. The dark circles beneath her eyes told me she might not be faring as well as she was letting on. I traced a single fingertip over the hollow under her eye. 'You sure you've been okay?'

She swallowed, stiffening under my touch. 'I can't do this again, I'm sorry.'

'I am too.' I cupped her jaw, leaning closer to place a soft kiss against her mouth.

She let out a tiny whimper, and a pulse of desire shot straight down my spine. God, why did I have to fuck up with her? She was perfect. She hadn't yet pushed me away so I leaned in again and met her mouth, this time parting her lips to taste her. My tongue sought hers out, not satisfied until she returned my kiss. She might have been mad at me, but her body still responded like I remembered—sensual and needy. Fuck, I was already hard.

I pushed my hips into hers, pinning her against the wall and brushed my erection up against her belly.

She brought her hands to my chest and pushed me back. 'I can't.' Her voice was weak, but her eyes were determined.

I wanted to push her, and knew I probably could. But she'd probably hate me even more in the morning if I did that. 'What can I do?' I asked.

'There's nothing you can do.' She stepped around me and left the stall, leaving me rock hard and sorely disappointed at the sight of her walking away from me yet again.

Why my bed suddenly felt so cold and empty without Alexa was beyond me. I normally had no trouble sleeping, typically falling exhausted into bed each night and sleeping soundly until morning. Now I lay in bed, watching the blades of my ceiling fan turn, wondering if I'd done the right thing letting her walk away. I didn't know if she would have listened if I'd tried to stop her. And hell, putting myself in her shoes, I would not be okay with her shooting porn.

Since Alexa had been gone, food had lost its flavor. Days blended into weeks. And it felt like I couldn't do a single thing right when it came to Lily anymore. I had no idea what was so difficult about making meatballs, but Lily made sure to point out I was doing it wrong—that this wasn't how Lexa did it—with that, and with other things too.

My one attempt at letting Alexa know I was still thinking of her was met with silence. The idea struck me when I'd passed by that bakery she and Lily liked. I'd bought a single white cupcake topped with a thick layer of pink frosting and I'd had it gift wrapped and delivered to her. The card had simply read *I miss you, cupcake.*

My house felt empty and cold without her in it. Lily noticed it too, I know she did, but we both forged on, despite the crushing weight of Alexa's loss. I alternated my time between work and the gym, needing an escape from my own house after Lily went to bed. The memories of sitting with Alexa after putting Lily to bed were too much. I could barely look at my damn couch without remembering all the naughty things I'd done to her in that very spot.

The mindless activity of pushing my muscles to the limit dispelled the swirling thoughts of her, if only for a little while. As soon as I was alone in the quiet shower after my workout, she was right back there with me in my mind. The sweet scent of her, her big blue eyes, her mischievous crooked smile. My cupcake.

I let the hard spray of water beat down my back, and grabbed the bar of soap. I washed my chest, under my arms, and my stomach, before my hands trailed lower. With thoughts of Alexa occupying my brain, my cock jumped to life. *Don't do it, man,* I warned. I didn't want to jerk myself off to the memory of her slipping down on her knees and flicking her wicked little tongue out to taste me before sucking me deep into the cavern of her warm mouth. The memory was too much. But I couldn't help it. I pictured her sweet face, that full mouth and the way she whimpered whenever I uttered a dirty endearment to her. My soapy hand found my shaft and began pumping. Hard and fast, needing release from the haunting memories of her. I leaned one hand against the shower wall, the spray of water pounding against my spine, and closed my eyes. 'Lex,' I whispered as the hot jets erupted from me and fell to the tiled floor.

Chapter 20

Alexa

The fall passed by quickly and by the first snowfall in December, my heart had begun to heal, though I knew I'd never forget Cade. Or Lily, for that matter. I still missed them both terribly, but my pride wouldn't let me contact him. He'd made his choice. In some aspects, it was the same pattern as how I grew up. My dad chose work over me and my mom too many times to count. Only with Cade's job, the betrayal was that much more devastating.

Over the past few weeks, I'd somehow fallen into the routine of actively dating Peter. Maybe it was because he was easy to be around and alleviated the feeling of being alone, or maybe because it made my mother so ridiculously happy, but whatever the reason, I was now going out with him several times a week. He'd taken me horseback riding and out for casual brunches and fancier dinners. He'd even come to a Sunday dinner at the club at my mother's insistence.

I spent the Christmas holiday in Aspen with my parents, skiing, eating too much and visiting the spa. It was a nice holiday, but of course, even there—halfway across the country—I couldn't keep my thoughts from Cade and Lily. Especially after he sent me a cupcake along with a note that stated he missed me only a few days before I left. I spent the first several days in Aspen glued to my cell phone, sure he was going to call. But the call never came. Perhaps the holidays and first snowfall of the year had made him sentimental, that was all. Yet I found myself lying in bed awake at night, wondering if I should have sent Lily a gift for Christmas, or if Cade cooked them Christmas dinner. For some reason, it depressed me to think of the two of them sitting around his small kitchen table with a meal of scrambled eggs and chicken wings. I wondered if they liked lobster, which was what my parents and I had. It didn't matter. I needed to get them out of my head. When I returned from Aspen, I would throw myself back into my regular routine, including seeing Peter again.

My first Saturday back from Aspen, Peter had arranged for us to see a matinee performance of The Nutcracker and was due any minute to pick me up.

I dressed in a merlot-colored sweater dress, heather-gray tights and my brown knee-high boots, leaving my hair down around my shoulders. I watched from the front window for Peter's car. I usually jogged out to meet him at the curb, since I preferred not to have him alone in my apartment. Though I liked spending time with him, I wasn't ready to go anywhere near the physical side of things again, with him or anyone. But so far, Peter had been very patient, settling for quick goodnight pecks in his car when he dropped me off.

I slid into his Lexus, and he leaned across the console and gave my cheek a quick kiss. 'You look nice. How was Aspen?'

'It was nice. Lots of time on the slopes with my dad and lots of spa time with my mom.' I left it at that. It felt a little strange to talk to Peter about my parents since he worked for my dad, but he didn't press for details. He was dressed in a chunky knit sweater, and I couldn't help but snicker. It wasn't the kind of thing a man would pick out and had to be a Christmas gift from his mom. I settled back in my seat and tried to relax, to just enjoy the day for what it was. I still hadn't gotten used to his car's new-car smell. It overwhelmed my senses, like he was pumping it in through the vents.

We drove in silence toward the theatre, and I found myself yawning. The sleepless nights over the past few weeks had caught up with me. 'Do you mind if we stop for a coffee before the show?'

He glanced at the clock on his dash. 'If we make it quick, it should be fine.'

A few minutes later, I pointed out the green sign of the coffee chain coming up at the next exit.

Peter pulled off the highway and into the parking lot, navigating to the drive-thru lane, which was backed up by a traffic jam of coffee seekers.

I counted the cars ahead of us. Seven. 'Shoot.'

Peter slid the gearshift into park and let out a sigh.

I slipped off my seatbelt. 'I'll just run inside. It'll be faster.'

'Alexa, we're already in line.' He glanced in the rearview mirror. 'And now I'm blocked in.'

'Don't worry, it'll be like a race. You wait here and I'll go inside.'

'A race, huh?' He grinned.

I nodded, and hopped out of the car. 'Yes. And I'll win. Be right back.'

Once inside, I noticed there were only two people ahead of me at the counter. Piece of cake. I contemplated my order, remembering that Peter liked hot chocolate with whipped cream, when the sound of rich, male laughter met my ears from across the room. There was something strikingly familiar about it and panic rose in my stomach. I reluctantly turned and spotted Cade seated at a small round table across from a woman.

I wished I could hide, that the floor would open and swallow me whole, but of course that didn't happen. He hadn't yet noticed me.

There was still a chance I could get away without being seen, but I couldn't resist one more glance. Cade was exactly as I remembered, all hard muscle and masculine features, a shadow of beard growth dusting his jaw. He leaned forward, resting his elbows on the table, listening intently to the woman. I could only see her profile, but she looked familiar and my mind worked to place her. Was she one of the babysitters he used? Something about the auburn hair hanging down her back had my mind working overtime. It didn't matter. I needed to get out of here.

I took a step back and knocked right into a tower of reindeer mugs, rattling the display.

Cade chose that exact moment to look up. His eyes settled on mine and a line creased his brow. 'Alexa?' He was on his feet and heading toward me before I could even contemplate escaping. 'What are you doing here?'

'Cade,' I mumbled incoherently, meeting his concerned gaze.

'Yeah. It's Cade.' He pressed a palm to my cheek. 'You okay? You look a little flushed.'

My eyes darted back across the room to the redhead at his table. She had turned to watch us, and her seeing her full on, I instantly knew who she was. My knees trembled and a wave of nausea crashed through me. Cade was on a date with the girl from his first film shoot. Desiree I think. I reminded myself to breathe, but little good it did me. My head was swimming with this discovery. Was she the reason he chose his work over me? How long had they been seeing each other outside of work?

Cade glanced back at the woman, and bit out a clipped apology. 'Sorry. Let me introduce you to Sara.' He motioned her over.

Sara? I supposed Desiree was her stage name.

When she rose from the table, her hand moved to cradle her swollen round belly and realization struck. She was several months pregnant. My legs went out from under me.

When I came to, I was lying on the floor. Cade was holding my head in his lap, sweeping his fingers across my forehead. My hazy eyes met his concerned ones.

'Cupcake?' he asked.

I moved to sit up, but his large hands on my shoulders held me in place. 'Stay put. You took quite a spill. You hit your head on the floor before I could catch you.' He rubbed the back of my head, massaging the swollen lump beneath my hair.

'Ouch.' I winced at the contact.

'That's what I thought.'

When I remembered what had sent me crashing to the floor in the first place—seeing Sara's pregnant belly—a sob broke free from the back of my throat and I struggled to free myself from Cade's grasp. I didn't want him holding me, trying to comfort me right now. Not to mention, I could see that I was causing quite the commotion in the coffee shop, sprawled out across the floor the way I was. Cade waved away a barista who was headed in our direction, her expression one of concern. 'I've got her.'

'Cade, let me up.'

He opened his mouth to argue, but the determination in my eyes had to have convinced him. He helped me up from the floor and sat me down in a leather chair in front of the fireplace. I wiped fresh tears from both cheeks, but the effort was futile. The tears refused to stop.

Sara was hovering by his side, and I heard Cade ask her to go get some tissues for me. She scurried off for the restrooms.

Peter came strolling into the coffee shop. 'Alexa, come on, we're going to be la—' He stopped in front me, looking down at my tear-streaked face. 'Alexa?'

Shit. I'd completely forgotten about Peter. I took the tissues from Sara and pressed them to my cheeks. So much for putting on mascara today. Cade knelt down beside my chair, taking the tissues from me to help mop up the tears.

'Alexa…? What's wrong? And who is this guy?' Peter asked.

'I'm sorry, Peter,' I managed. 'This is Cade.'

Peter's eyes went to Cade's kneeling form and a look of disbelief overtook his face. 'This guy?'

Peter didn't know much about Cade, just that he was the guy I'd been seeing before him, and that he was the reason I didn't want anything to do with a relationship right now because of the rocky way things had ended between us. I could see Peter's surprise that I'd dated a guy like Cade at all—scruffy, worn jeans, work boots and a fitted long-sleeve pullover that emphasized his over-muscled chest made him the polar opposite of Peter's gelled hair, tweed blazers and Italian-leather loafers. I blew my nose, knowing I looked like a mess and long past caring. I felt like I'd been hit by a train.

Cade looked between Peter and I. 'I'm taking her home,' he informed us both.

I squeaked out a protest, and Peter took a step closer. But Cade rose to his feet, towering over us both. He turned to Sara, placed a hand on her belly, and leaned in toward her to whisper something in her ear.

A pain stabbed at my chest.

Peter placed his hand on my shoulder, but turned to address Cade. 'You're not taking her anywhere. First of all, we're on a date. Second of all, I'm pretty sure you're the reason she's crying right now.'

Sara kissed Cade's cheek and headed for the door. I didn't blame her for disappearing. That sounded pretty appealing right about now.

'We don't have to go, Peter.' The last thing I wanted to do at this very moment was watch a ballet that included a sweet little love story.

'I, ah, didn't tell you before, Alexa, but I got these tickets from my uncle. We're joining him and his wife at the play.'

135

He'd tricked me into some weird family get-together? There was no way I was meeting his aunt and uncle right now—or ever.

'I just want to go home,' I murmured.

They both looked down at me.

'I'm taking her home,' Cade repeated.

Peter sighed. 'Fine. I've got to go or I'm going to be late. Are you sure you're okay with him taking you home?'

It wasn't like I had much of a choice—Peter was practically stranding me, miles away from home. 'It's fine. Just go, Peter.'

He leaned down and kissed the top of my head. 'I'll call you later.'

Don't bother, I uttered to myself.

I'd never been inside Cade's truck before. The cab was in need of a good cleaning, and there were water bottles littering the floor and a Cinderella coloring book on the seat between us. It smelled like a mix of his subtle cologne and the spicy scent of a man after a hard day's work.

He didn't say anything as we drove. He just stared straight ahead and rested one hand on top of the wheel.

When he pulled into my condo complex, I realized I hadn't provided my address, nor had he asked for directions. He parked next to my car and turned off the ignition.

We sat in silence for a few moments. Thankfully, my sobs had quieted into little hiccups. 'Thanks for bringing me home.' I pushed against the truck door, and climbed down carefully, realizing the ground was farther away than I thought.

He met me at the side of the truck and took my hand, stopping me. 'Wait. Let me explain.'

I don't know what possessed me, whether it was the closure I was craving, or my own morbid curiosity about his expectant girlfriend, but I nodded. I wrapped my arms around my middle, bracing myself for his explanation.

'Not here. Invite me inside, Lex.'

I nodded my consent and led him inside. I tossed my purse and keys onto the entryway table and made my way to the couch, not knowing how much longer my shaky legs would hold my weight. I collapsed and immediately curled myself into a ball. I expected Cade to be right behind me, but strangely, I heard him rummaging around inside my kitchen.

I lifted my head and watched him walk toward me carrying a glass of orange juice, a box of Kleenex and a bottle of pain reliever. He held out the glass of juice for me while he opened the bottle of pills. Only once I had swallowed a dose did he sit down beside me. His news had to be even worse than I imagined, since he was being so kind to me. Maybe Sara was pregnant with twins, or they were engaged. Crap, why hadn't I checked her left hand? Not that it mattered, I reminded myself.

I took a deep breath. 'So when is she due?'

His face twisted in confusion. 'Who, Sara?'

Obviously. I nodded.

'Ah, end of April, I think.'

'Well, I'm sorry about my reaction…it just took me by surprise.' I'd apologize for my public anxiety attack, but I drew the line at offering up my congratulations or breaking out the champagne.

Cade studied my features wearily and scrubbed a hand over the back of his neck. 'Damn, cupcake, the baby's not mine.'

Chapter 21

Cade

The little sobs that were still wracking her chest made me feel like a complete asshole. Alexa had broken down at the mere sight of me. But thinking I'd gotten one of my co-stars pregnant on top of that? Damn, I was just fucking up left and right. I needed to explain this to her, to get this right once and for all.

I took her hand in mine. 'Sara's boyfriend is the father. I only met up with her because she wanted my opinion about how I left the adult film business. Despite the fact that she's pregnant, Rick's still been harassing her about working for him.'

'Wait.' She pulled her hand away suddenly, her face scrunching up. 'The baby's not yours?'

'No. Not mine.' Thank fucking God. I knew I wasn't ready to bring a kid into this world. I had my hands full enough with Lil already. But the idea of watching Alexa's belly grow bigger with my baby... Well, that was a different story. I pushed the thought away.

'Oh.' Her shoulders sagged in relief. 'And...you left the business?'

'Yes. I never intended to be a porn star, Lex. I just had thousands of dollars in medical bills for Lily that I had no way of paying. I needed to make some fast money.' I wanted to tell her that was my plan all along and if she'd just let me explain myself that morning… but I bit my tongue. I hadn't even tried to stop her the morning that she left. And I'd regretted that every damn day since.

She closed her eyes and drew in a shaky breath. 'Oh,' she said again.

Though I knew I shouldn't, that it was none of my fucking business, I couldn't get that prick she'd been on a date with out of my head. 'Lex…' I inched closer to her on the couch, dropping my voice lower, 'that guy…Peter…has he touched you?'

Her eyes snapped open and met mine. 'Do you know what you're saying?' A tense silence hung in the air around us. 'We're dating, as in me and him. Not me and you. You don't get a say in who touches me.'

All right then. I guess that cleared that up. I'd fucked up royally with her. But the thought of someone else's hand on her made me want to hit something. Hard. 'For what it's worth, I am sorry about everything. Well, not everything. I wouldn't take back that night with you,' I admitted.

Her body went rigid. 'You're an asshole, you know that?' She stood and paced in front of the couch, seeming to draw strength from her anger—an anger that was currently being directed at me. 'If you needed money for Lily, all you had to do was ask.'

'Out of the question.' I shook my head. I didn't take handouts. Plain and simple. It was a promise I made myself when I took custody of Lily rather than having her end up in foster care. I would take full responsibility for her. End of story.

Alexa spun towards me, her hands landing on her hips. 'The fact that you could betray me that way—by sleeping with another woman rather than put your macho ego aside and ask for the money…' She wiped away the tears that had escaped the corners of her eyes. 'I can't forgive that…I can't get over it. I'm sorry.'

'I am, too.' I stood and kissed her forehead, before disappearing through the front door.

Fuck! The curse ripped through my chest as I peeled out of her complex. I slammed my hand against my dash, cursing as I accelerated toward home.

After driving around aimlessly until I got my heart rate under control, I was surprised to see an hour had passed. Being with her today, watching her break down, I knew there was no way in fuck I could walk away and forget her. I'd wanted to hold her, wipe away her tears, kiss away her sobs. But she wasn't mine anymore. And that realization was like a punch to the gut. Fuck it. I was not giving her up this easily.

Just the thought of going back home without her, back to my empty life, and waking up to an empty bed every morning... No. I wouldn't settle. Not this time. I wanted to see her lift Lily onto her hip again, make her giggle the way she had before. Maybe I wasn't worthy of her love, but I was just selfish enough to try.

I made a quick phone call, asking Sophia if she wouldn't mind staying with Lily a little longer. Hell, what I was about to do could take five minutes or all night if I had my way. I told Lily I loved her and to listen to Sophia.

'Love you, Caden!' her little voice rang in my ear.

'Love you too, baby girl.' Lily's faith in me calmed me more than a little bit, and I pulled a U-turn, anxious to get back to Lex.

I knocked at the door I had fled from just over an hour ago, but this time, my nerves were crackling. She'd made it clear she was no longer interested, but her tears told me there was more to it. She was still hurting, so maybe I still had a chance.

'Go away, Kenz!' Alexa's muffled voice called from inside. 'Vodka won't fix me this time.'

I knocked again. 'It's Cade.'

The door flew open. 'Cade?' She swayed on her feet and I reached out to steady her, gripping her upper arms. I couldn't seem to stop touching her, even though she practically winced each time I did so.

'Whoa. I've got you.' I needed to get my shit together, to find the right words to make her understand. But I'd never been good at romantic speeches, and I doubted that was going to change now. I'd just have to find a way, without words, to show her.

The sweet scent of her skin and her hazy blue eyes sent a streak of desire straight down my spine.

Fuuuck.

Chapter 22

Alexa

'Cade? What are you doing here?' I stepped back, out of his grasp. 'I called MacKenzie after you left and thought it was her coming to…come over.' I'd been about to say cheer me up, but doing so would have implied I was a complete wreck. I didn't want to give him that kind of power over me.

'Can I come in?'

My brain had apparently taken a leave of absence, because I stepped back, allowing him to enter. His musky scent washed over me, and I wanted nothing more than to bury my face in his neck and inhale. *No, Alexa. No.* Crap, maybe the three vodka shots I'd slammed in quick succession after he'd left hadn't been such a good idea. My hands were already shaking and I was struggling to remain upright.

I retreated into the kitchen and downed one more shot for good measure, before Cade entered the kitchen behind me. He recapped the bottle of vodka and placed it back inside the freezer.

'Enough,' he said roughly, his warm breath brushing over the back of my neck.

I leaned back against the kitchen island, his looming presence holding me captive. 'Why'd you come back?' I'd been hoping to sound suspicious, hardened, but instead my voice gave away my desperate and intoxicated state. *Damn.*

'Are you drunk?' He reached out and toyed with a lock of my hair. 'I was only gone an hour.' His hand brushed my cheek, lingering for just a moment.

I lifted my chin and smirked up at him. 'No comment.' He'd soon realize what a mess I was, regardless. Seeing him with Sara and thinking he had moved on… God, it had crushed me. Even finding out that he wasn't the baby's father hadn't eased my mind. It wasn't as though he was asking for me back…was he? And what would I say if he did?

I needed to be strong. And in my buzzed state, with Cade's masculine deliciousness standing in my kitchen, it was going to take a friggin' miracle.

I placed my hands on my hips. 'Why are you here, Cade?'

His gaze collided with mine. 'You.'

My throat tightened and I gripped the counter for support. Cade said nothing further and made no move toward me. He just continued watching me, his eyes growing dark with desire. The anticipation sent my heartbeat thudding erratically in my chest.

Surely he knew this wasn't fair. It would be beyond unfair to seduce me right now, when I was vulnerable and needy for his touch. I wanted so much more, but even before I processed it, I knew I would freely and willingly give him anything he wanted. Even knowing that my heart would surely shrivel up and disintegrate once and for all when he left me this time around.

He stepped in closer, as if testing the waters, and when I made no move to stop him, and in fact angled my body toward his, he closed the rest of the distance between us and hauled me up against him.

I sagged in relief. I'd missed this. The hard planes of his chest, his firm thighs pressing against mine in that familiar way. I'd missed *him* and at this point, I was desperate enough to take whatever I could get. My heart jumped into action, pounding against my ribs and my brain warred with my body. Could I handle the consequences of another night with Cade? He leaned down and planted a tender kiss on my jaw, just below my earlobe.

My heart said no, while my body screamed yes. Maybe if I purposely, knowingly chose this, if I was using *him* this time around… the loss wouldn't hurt as much. I steeled my nerves to take what I needed from him…one last time. I needed to be the one in control.

I captured his mouth in a crushing kiss, parting his lips with my tongue and eagerly swirling my tongue with his.

His hands came up to cup my jaw, tilting my head to deepen the kiss. While his hands tangled in my hair and caressed my cheek, I didn't allow myself to feel the tenderness of the moment, and instead took charge, unbuttoning his jeans and working my hand inside. His cock stiffened under my none-too-gentle ministrations and once he was fully hard, I broke away from the kiss and dropped to my knees in front of him.

Cade chuckled, bringing his hand down to pet my hair, smoothing it back from my face. 'Damn, baby, you in a hurry?'

But his laughter died on his lips when my mouth crested around his swollen head, pulling him deep inside.

'Oh, fuck.'

Pride swelled within me and I put every ounce of energy I had into the performance. My mind replayed the images from his videos, and I mimicked the moves I'd seen—licking his balls and sucking one of them into my mouth. Cade flinched and pulled back. 'You don't like it?' I asked, looking up at him with wide eyes.

His eyes blazed down at mine. 'It's…okay.' He seemed to struggle for the right words. He stroked my hair back from my face, while trying to read my expression. 'I like you sucking on my cock better, that's all.'

'Oh. But in your last video…' I stopped, snapping my mouth closed.

Realization crossed his features, and it seemed we were both remembering the way he pulled himself free from the girl's mouth and directed her to his balls. He stroked his thumb along my jaw. 'That was just for the camera, baby. It was acting. My cock is yours, and there was something that didn't feel right about her doing that. My last memories were of you sucking me deep into your throat, and I didn't want anyone else's lips around me right then. I know that probably sounds stupid to you, considering… But it's the truth.'

I took a deep breath. It didn't matter what he said at this point, I reminded myself. He couldn't make this right. I needed to be strong. 'Kay. Got it.' I returned to my task, gripping him firmly with both hands as I stroked and suckled at the same time, forcing all thoughts away from my mind.

'Damn, cupcake.' His knees trembled, and his hands wound their way into my hair, lifting it from my face and arranging it in a ponytail behind my head.

With one hand still planted in my hair, he gripped his shaft in his other hand and pulled himself free from my mouth. 'I don't want to come yet,' he said through gritted teeth. 'Let me take care of you.'

He grabbed my upper arms, pulling me to my feet, and planted a series of sweet kisses on my mouth.

'No. I need you inside me. Now.' He read the insistence in my eyes.

'Okay.' He pulled the hem of my sweater dress up and I lifted my arms, suddenly standing before him in just my bra and panties.

I reached around to unclasp my bra ditching it and then quickly removed my panties. I wasn't sure why, but I needed to be in control. Not bothering to remove Cade's shirt, I pulled him in toward me, my back pressed against the counter. His eyes held a trace of hesitation, but I pulled his lips to mine. 'Take me.'

He lifted me onto the counter and rubbed at the lips of my swollen sex. 'Are you wet enough, sweetheart? I don't want to hurt you.'

He needed to cut it out with this nice guy shit. We both knew he wasn't. This was exactly why my heart was in shreds.

Finding that I was already soaking wet—damn hormones—he rolled on a condom taken from his wallet. I wrapped my legs around his waist and dug my heels into his ass, urging him forward. Seconds later I felt his cock nudging at my entrance. Yes, this was what I needed, just to forget about everything else and lose myself in the sensations. A wave of desire raced through my belly.

He inched forward, slipping inside me slowly. Achingly slowly.

I arched my back, lying against the cool hard counter, and squeezed my eyes closed. 'Harder. Fuck me harder.'

Cade's movements picked up, if only infinitesimally, and his fingertips grazed my breasts. 'Alexa? Look at me.'

I opened one eye. 'Just do it Cade. You're not going to break me.'

His hands moved to my hips to pull me forward against his pelvis. I watched his movements for a moment before letting my eyes drift closed again. I rocked my hips against his, despite the pleasure-pain combo gripping my insides from the fullness. I let out heavy pants, pushing my hips forward in time to meet his thrusts, cutting into his ass with my fingernails.

'Stop, Lex, stop. This isn't revenge sex.' He pulled away from me, his cock, warm and wet, resting against my belly. 'What are you doing?' He took my shoulders, gently shaking them until I met his gaze.

I sat up on the counter, tears welling in my eyes. What the hell was I doing? This wasn't me. I wasn't a goddess in the bedroom—or kitchen, as it were—I was inexperienced and clumsy. I was only doing this because my feelings for him terrified me. I loved him. I fucking loved him. I sucked in my bottom lip, refusing to cry. 'I'm not a porn star. I know I'm not like the other women you've been with…'

He released a frustrated breath, and clenched his fists at his sides. 'That's what you thought this was? That I wanted rough sex with you...because of my past...' He yanked up his boxers and jeans. 'Fuck.' The curse ripped through his chest in a low growl. His hands were trembling and the look in his eyes was unlike anything I'd ever seen.

I pulled in a shaky breath.

Cade scooped me up from the counter, easily lifting me in his arms, and cradled me against his chest as he stalked from the kitchen. He kicked open the door to my bedroom and tossed me in the center of the bed, where I landed with a soft thud.

He crawled towards me, leaning in close to my ear, his voice low and laced with anger. 'If you want me to fuck you hard, I will. But not because you think it's what I want. I want you. Just you, Alexa. Your soft curves, your lack of experience, your tight pussy that's only ever been mine. That night with you, despite what I might have said, we made love, and it was the best sex of my life.' He sat back on his heels, giving me a chance to process his words. 'And more than that, it wasn't just sex that we shared that night.' He rubbed his hands over his hair. 'Christ, cupcake. I'm in love with you.'

Chapter 23

Cade

Alexa's stunned reaction to those five little words wasn't quite what I was expecting. Her wide blue eyes stayed locked on mine for several seconds before they pinched closed. She shook her head. 'Don't say it if you don't mean it.'

I cupped her cheeks, and she opened her eyes. 'I meant every word. I love you.' A smile blossomed on her lips and I leaned forward to kiss her. 'If I have to sacrifice to give you everything you want, if I have to change who I am, whatever I have to do—tell me. It's done. I can't believe I thought I could live without you.'

She looked down, a rosy blush staining her cheeks. 'Cade,' she whispered softly, gripping handfuls of the sheets in her little palms.

'I was fucking miserable without you. An absolute wreck. Please forgive me, cupcake.'

She looked up, seeming to draw some strength at hearing me grovel, her mischievous grin slipping back in place. 'And you'll commit—only to me. No more filming no matter how tough times get.'

'I promise.' I kissed the back of her hand, her knuckles, her wrist.

'And you won't even so much as look at another woman when we're together.'

I met her eyes. 'I won't need to. I've got the most beautiful girl in the world with me.' We were making our own vows to each

148

other, and no matter how strange they might have seemed they were perfect for us. 'Will you be okay with me sitting on my ass on Sunday afternoons, watching the game and having a beer?'

She laughed, deep and throaty. 'Only if you'll let me have chicken wings.'

I smirked. 'Done.'

She crawled onto my lap, straddling me and resting her head against my chest. It was strange how I'd come to think of this as her spot. She traced a tender fingertip lightly over my chest, grazing against the hair. 'Would you go to the store and get me tampons and chocolate ice cream and cheesy gossip magazines when I need them?'

'Damn baby, if I can play Beauty Shop Barbie with Lil, don't you think I can handle that?'

She chuckled, her chest brushing against mine as she laughed. My body stirred to life, remembering that we were still mostly naked.

I turned and gently lowered her onto the bed, settling myself over her. I licked her nipples, pulling one into my mouth, and kept my eyes locked on hers. I took my time, thoroughly worshipping her with my mouth and fingers until she was soaking wet and begging me for more. God, I loved this girl.

I arranged her on her back, her legs spread wide for me, and knelt between her knees. I inched forward until I was disappearing inside her. Watching my cock slip between her pink folds was insanely hot.

My only issue with this position, propped up on my knees the way I was, was that I couldn't kiss her. I had the perfect view of her hot little body, however, so I used it to my full advantage. Having her laid out before me this way allowed me to cup her breasts and dip between her legs to massage her clit. 'I want you to come for me, baby.'

She moaned softly, her eyes closing in concentration. 'Cade, I want it faster.'

'You sure, baby?'

'Yeah,' she groaned out, meeting my gaze again.

I gripped her knees and increased my tempo, until I was fully buried with each thrust, my balls hitting her ass.

Oh fuck, I wasn't going to last at this pace. Her warmth, her body, her tight little pussy…. Ah, shit. 'Baby, I'm going to come.'

'Not yet,' she whispered.

I bit back a curse, and pumped harder, circling her clit faster. Droplets of sweat rolled down my back from the effort of holding off my orgasm. 'Baby?'

'Not yet,' she cried.

I gripped the base of my shaft, pinching off my impending orgasm, and continued thrusting. My balls tightened as the physical ache from holding back overtook me.

Her cries got louder and her hips ground against mine. She was close. With one hand still playing with her clit, I used my other to massage one breast, pinching and rubbing her swollen nipples.

Her hips shot off the bed and her raspy voice moaning my name sent me over the edge. I pumped twice more and climaxed, leaning over her to whisper loving endearments while I came.

We made love twice more and then called for delivery, refusing to get out of bed even while we ate—sushi of all things. Alexa had promised I'd like it, and surprisingly it actually wasn't half bad. Once we finished, we lounged in the center of the bed, unwilling to leave each other's arms.

'How could I be enough for you, baby? You deserve the world. My own parents didn't even want me,' I asked, tracing a single fingertip over her naked hipbone. I'd denied her request to get dressed after the last time we'd made love.

She leaned up on her elbow to look down at me. 'Your parents missed out on an amazing man. And as far as you not being good enough…' She shook her head. 'Think about the unconditional love you have for Lily. She may have her challenges, and you probably never envisioned caring for a six year old at your age, but to you, she's perfect.'

I knew she was right. I'd take a bullet for Lily. And I felt the same way about Alexa.

'You might not have been who I ever pictured myself with, but you're exactly what I need—someone I can let loose and be myself with. Not some uptight, suit-wearing douchebag who's only hanging around in the hopes of impressing my father to secure his next promotion.'

'True. That's not me.'

'And I love that about you. I love knowing that you'd stand up to my parents—or anyone, for that matter—to make sure I was happy.'

'Hell, yeah, I would.'

I tucked Lex under my arm and held her until her breathing became deep and even. I hadn't ever spent the night away from Lily, but knowing Sophia was sleeping over at my place, and that Lily was safe—and most importantly that I had Alexa back—I fell into an easy sleep, feeling happier and more complete than I ever had.

'What exactly do you think you're doing?' I asked Alexa as she crawled across the cab of my truck and onto my lap.

'Shh. I have an idea,' she murmured against my neck. Having her straddling my hips in that little black skirt sent a wave of desire through my system.

'No fair, baby. I don't have room to touch you.' I gripped the arm rests on either side of her, caging her in against me, but still letting her have her way.

She lifted her chin and caught my eyes, confidence and desire blazing in those blue depths. 'Hush. I was once told you liked sex in the cab of your truck.'

A low rich chuckle tumbled from my lips. *That's what this was?* 'Used to. Pre-Alexa.' Or P.A., as we'd taken to calling my life before her. I was not fucking her in my truck. Sure it was dark out and the parking lot was mostly deserted, given the hour, but Alexa deserved more. She deserved everything.

She grinned at me, nestling herself in even more snugly in my lap. 'Yes, but you came out dancing with my friends tonight even though I know you hate loud clubs, and I want to reward you.' She rocked her hips against the front of my jeans, the friction of our bodies demanding attention.

I took her chin in my hand and kissed her mouth. I did hate dance clubs, but getting to watch Alexa dance in a miniskirt and heels and feeling her grind up against me all night, well let's just say I was no martyr. It had also helped that we'd seemed to bridge the gap between our friends, inviting several of her friends and mine out together. Sort of our first real coming out as a couple. And to our surprise, everyone had gotten along well. Even Tyson and I had buried the hatchet between us. It appeared some had gotten along better than others, too—case in point, I was pretty sure Ian and MacKenzie were currently en route to his place.

I couldn't help but smile, because this was exactly what we'd been doing for the past month—her introducing me to the things in her world and me introducing her to mine.

Alexa continued to watch me, her expression curious, her mouth curving into a mischievous smile.

'Not here. Not in my truck, baby. Let me take you home where I can fuck you properly,' I kissed her, nipping at her mouth.

She grinned and shook her head. 'I'm not breakable, Cade. You don't have to treat me like a princess. I want you.'

'Cupcake…' my voice came out in a half moan, half whisper.

She worked her hands in between us, unbuckling my belt and tugging down my jeans. God, I was completely at her mercy. She owned me. And the gleam in her eye and smile twitching on her lips told me she knew it.

'I think I need to remind you…' She tugged my boxers down just enough to free my cock. 'That this belongs to me.' She angled herself closer, grinding against me so I could feel just how damp her panties were.

Fuuuuck. 'Oh, it's all yours, cupcake.' I tugged her panties to the side, running my thumb along her swollen lips. Knowing she was ready, I thrust my hips up, meeting her wet heat with gentle thrusts. She whimpered and writhed, adjusting to the fullness as I slipped inside. I clenched my jaw to keep from crying out when her impossibly tight, warm channel sank down on me.

'Every inch, mine,' she whispered.

'Yes, yours.' I kissed her passionately while she increased her speed.

Alexa cried out and pressed her hand against the window, smearing the steamed-up glass with a handprint. If it wasn't obvious what was happening in this truck before, it certainly was now.

Her whimpers grew more insistent and I knew she was close. I never had to ask her anymore. I could always tell when she was about to come and timed my release accordingly. She raised and lowered herself on me while repeatedly moaning my name like it was her mantra. It was fucking hot. She tossed her head back, moaning low in her throat and rode out the pulsing orgasm I could feel squeezing me. I gripped her hips, pumping hard and fast, and quickly followed her over the edge.

After, I cradled her to my chest, holding her while our heartbeats slowed and breaths mingled. 'I love you, cupcake.'

'I love you, Caden,' she murmured, her lips pressed against my neck.

Epilogue

Alexa ~ Eight months later

'That girl's a fish—look at her go,' my dad chuckled, squinting into the sun.

Watching Lily splash around in the pool was my new favorite way to spend a Saturday. I had grown up in this pool, on the patio of this Country Club, but somehow watching Lily enjoy it was even better than my own memories.

My mom was in the pool with Lily, since trying to keep her out of the water was like trying to keep Cade from calling me cupcake—it was a lost cause.

I looked across the terrace to find Cade returning with lunch. He set the foam boxes on the table between my father and I, before dropping a kiss on my lips and settling in the lounge chair beside me.

'What's for lunch?' my dad asked, addressing Cade.

He chuckled. 'Burgers. What else?'

It had becoming a running joke between them. When my mom wasn't in the pool with Lily and was the one to order lunch, she'd come back with salmon salad or something equally as foreign to Cade and Lily's palates. They were good sports about it though, just like my parents were when Cade came back with cheeseburgers for everyone. It was like we were all learning to exist together.

Even my dad had cut back on working Saturdays in the summer to spend the days with us here.

Things had changed considerably over the past several months since I graduated from nursing school. Most notably, Cade had won my parents over. It hadn't been easy at first, but Cade had persisted. He'd started his own successful contracting company, and sought my dad out for financial advice, which he was all too happy to provide, seeing as finance was his favorite topic. My dad in turn referred him to several clients for remodeling projects— wealthy people at the country club—and Cade's business had grown considerably in a short time. Most of all, it gave him a boost of confidence, and forced any lingering worries over money from his mind. It was nice to see him a bit more relaxed because of it.

Another big part of my parents coming around had to do with little Lily—she was just so loveable. Though my mom never seemed the grandmotherly type, she'd begun coming over several days a week to pick up Lily. It was nice to see my mother have someone in her life to devote attention to, rather than sitting alone in their big house.

Cade had begun helping my dad around the house with odds and ends, my father gaining a healthy respect for the self-taught skills Cade possessed. Of course we'd conveniently left out Cade's brief stint as a porn star and though his videos were still online, we doubted my parents would ever discover them.

The biggest change came last month when Cade sold his grandparents' little house, and I sold the condo my parents had bought for me a few years before, and together we bought a house halfway between both our places. It was in the same school district for Lily and still close to the hospital, where I now worked full time.

My dad grabbed a towel for my mom and Lily's pink hooded towel that had her name embroidered along one side—a gift from my mom—and helped them from the pool.

I took the opportunity to inspect Cade. His eyes were glued to me too.

Cade in a pair of navy swim trunks slung low on his hips was enough to make me want to drop my bikini bottoms and wade out in the water with him for some underwater action, spectators be damned. But of course, I didn't. I just clenched my thighs together, knowing that when we got home from the pool, Lily would be exhausted and ready for a nap and Cade and I could disappear into our room for some alone time.

'Later cupcake,' Cade whispered as if reading my mind. 'Now eat. You're going to need your energy for what I have planned.'

I stifled a gasp and grinned up at him. I was his, completely. Body, heart and soul. And I wouldn't want it any other way.

Acknowledgements

To my girls—both Courtneys and my little muse, Sammy Rae. Thank you for your unending support and love on this journey, even when your own dating adventures have the distinct possibility of appearing in a book at some point.

Thank you once again my fabulous editor, Tanya Saari, who has knocked my socks off with her ability to polish my story into a novel. Thank you, my dear.

A special thanks goes out to my critique partners: Madison Seidler, Lolita Verroen and Charlie Evans. Thank you for your thoughtful advice. The dangerous duo of Sali Powers and Jenny Aspinall are in a critiquing category all their own, purely for the astounding number of exclamation points and F-bombs dropped when telling me what they liked or didn't about the book. You two are getting characters named in honor of you in my next book. Just wait!! Love ya, gals!

A giant bear hug goes out to my readers for believing in my stories and letting me entertain you. I love connecting with you on Facebook, Twitter, and GoodReads. You make this so much fun!

Oh, and to my sexy husband who might just be my biggest fan of all. Hi sweetie!

www.ingramcontent.com/pod-product-compliance
Ingram Content Group UK Ltd.
Pitfield, Milton Keynes, MK11 3LW, UK
UKHW020844190325
456436UK00005B/150